TOR'S SAGA

ALSO BY RON BRIGGS

Yellow Hair Series

Erik Haraldsson

TOR'S SAGA

YELLOW HAIR
BOOK TWO

RON BRIGGS

WOLFPACK
PUBLISHING
— EST 2013 —

Tor's Saga
Paperback Edition
Copyright © 2024 (As Revised) Ron Briggs

Wolfpack Publishing
1707 E. Diana Street
Tampa, Florida 33609

wolfpackpublishing.com

Paperback ISBN 978-1-63977-656-6
eBook ISBN 978-1-63977-655-9

FOREWORD

This is a work of fiction. The characters, events, and places are contrived by the author. An honest attempt has been made to describe real cultures and interactions as they may have taken place early in the eleventh century.

The cultures depicted in this story are the Norwegian Norse, Greenlandic Norse, Icelandic Norse, riverine Lenni Lenape, Monongahela, Late Fort Ancient, Ilini, and Owasco or proto-Iroquois (also called Haudenosaunee by some).

The descriptions reflect the transition from Middle to Late Woodland Period traditions and touch on the blossoming of the Mississippian culture that would have a great influence over the next several generations all across North America.

This second book of the *Yellow Hair* series tells

Tor's story. The son of Erik Haraldsson, Tor is the lone survivor of a shipwreck that leaves him stranded on a beach where he is discovered by a Lenni Lenape family. The boy grows into a man in the Lenape lands, but word of his arrival reaches the Mississippi, and he is bound for Cahokia.

TOR'S SAGA

CHAPTER I
REALITY

T or gently eased the hook from the fish's lip, then struggled to keep it from flopping out of his hands and back into the water. He slipped two fingers into a gill slit. "This thing must weigh a stone and a half! It is the biggest one I have ever caught!" he exclaimed. Then, he untied the cord with the other fish he had caught and added this one. "Father will be proud of me, and mother will be happy that there is plenty of succulent trout for the evening meal." It was still early morning. He set his pole aside, and lay back in the soft, green grass, letting the babbling creek play its lullaby as he drifted toward dreamland.

This high meadow is my favorite place in the entire world! From here, I can look down on the hill with Father's great hall, its big rock barn, and other *outbuildings. I can make out the trail that winds down through the sparse trees to the shipworks and smithy that stand just above the high-tide line on the stony beach. I can picture the knorrs and longships I have worked on along that shore.*

Just up the fjord from the shipworks are the large wooden docks that serve Ulfrstadt. At any given time, a person might see boats ranging from one-man rowboats to large fishing boats and coastal traders to knorrs of all sizes, including the big ocean-going ships that transport goods and people to and from the outside world. Occasionally, even a dragon, or longship, would be moored there—several of them if a great raid or war were about to begin.

From here, the most prominent feature in the village is the Christian church, its tall, dark bell tower rising high above the houses and shops. It is younger than my twelve winters.

Ulfrstadt, Ulfrfjord, and Ulfrland were renamed by great-great-great-grandfather, Arg Ulfrsson, after he was given the rank of jarl and granted the land by the new king, Harald Finehair, for Arg's contributions in the uniting of Norway under one king. Tor pictured the man as a huge, wild-eyed 'berserker.' Family legend has it that Arg Ulfrson's father was a weak, no-account farmer, and that Arg was the offspring of a wolf that had mated with his mother. Thus, he claimed the name Arg Ulfrson. And he fought like a wolf, with cunning and ferocity. The eldest male in his family had been jarl of Ulfrland ever since. Father had been known as Jarl Erik Haraldsson until he passed the title to Sven, his younger brother.

To the south and east of the village, Tor could picture the peat bogs. Further up the fjord is the hill where Tor's great-uncle Haakon had built his hall...

"Wait—something is wrong! I am lying on a hard floor, not soft meadow grass...and the stream is just 'hissing,' not tumbling over rocks," Tor scolded himself. Reluctantly, he forced his eyes open...and reality came crashing down on him like the tall oak trees they felled to cut and shape keel boards for the great longships they had built. His dream vanished like a puff of smoke in a strong wind.

He was alone, completely alone, the sole survivor of the wrecked *Sea Ox*, the great knorr they had built for their emigration voyage to Greenland. "How did it come to this?" he asked, looking to the sky, hoping to see God's image. "Why am I alive when everyone else has perished?" he demanded, his eyes filling with moisture.

CHAPTER 2
BAD MEMORIES

The voyage had gone smoothly until Iceland came into sight. Suddenly a violent storm attacked them, and drove their great ship far from Iceland, or any other land mass. Storm after storm ravaged their damaged ship. Most people died. Eventually, only four seasoned sailors and Tor were left aboard the ill-fated ship.

More than one 140 men, women, and children had left Ulfrstadt for the opportunities Greenland offered. On two ships, they carried their meager belongings along with their hopes and dreams for a prosperous new life. The hardened sailors saw the trip as a chance to be where they loved to be—at sea.

Now, Tor was alone. Everyone else was dead.

"Why me, Lord!?" he rasped, his voice and strength having long since abandoned him.

He was floating on a deck board. He knew exactly which one, for he had driven the long nails that held it in place. It had been the center board on the small, raised aft deck, behind the steerboard. He had been trying to sleep on that deck, even as that last storm raged.

The events came back to him in vivid detail. Tor recalled Gunnar telling Einar when he took the steerboard that the ship felt heavier. Einar called Bjarni and Gorm from their fruitless effort to bale water from the hold.

The latest storm was raging, driving them westward through waves higher than the ship was long. The older crew members thought Tor was asleep, but they had to yell as they appraised their situation. They concluded there was nothing for it. The ship was taking water faster than they could bale. They were sinking.

When the men went to wake Tor, he informed them that he was awake and had heard everything. The end was upon them. The sound of waves breaking on a rocky shoal loomed just ahead, sounding louder than the crashing thunder, and howling wind of the storm. The first hit was just a shuddering jar as they slid to the bottom of a trough. The next wave lifted them high, and when the great ship slid back down into the next trough, the collision had caused it to finally succumb to the power of the sea.

The jarring crash was followed by the sickening sound of wood splintering and rivets popping. Just then, a huge wave broke over the stern and carried Tor overboard and into the roaring, thrashing sea. The wave carried Tor over the jagged rock ridge that made up the crest of the shoal. It took all his strength to get his head above water to take an occasional breath. After floundering in the thrashing water for an unknown amount of time, Tor saw in a flash of lightning, the deck board coming straight toward him. Somehow, he managed to catch it and crawl onto the thick pine plank. He knew that board, had helped to cut, shape, smooth, and waterproof it before nailing it into place.

The lightning continued to flash, thunder rolled continuously, and rain slashed relentlessly. But the roar of the waves breaking over the shoal began to fade as he was carried away from it. Tor heard no shouts from the four sailors who had become like older brothers to him. Now they, along with most of the people he knew in all the world, were dead, leaving him alone and lost somewhere in the middle of a great sea.

Tor broke down and sobbed as he desperately

clung to the deck board, which was a little more than twice his length, just wider than his shoulders, and five fingers thick. Lost in his hysterics, Tor failed to notice the fading storm and calming seas. Sometime during the night, he cried himself to sleep.

CHAPTER 3

HOPELESSNESS

After a restless night, Tor awoke midmorning. The sun had risen over storm clouds drifting to the southeast, and the seas had calmed to low, rolling ripples that barely made his board bob. Tor felt completely drained. He had not eaten anything since the last storm descended on the hapless ship.

When was that? A day, or five days, past? He could not recall. *How long did I sleep?* He had no way of knowing.

That storm had driven them west-southwest for two days and nights before they heard the roar of waves breaking on the shoal over the din of constant thunder. It was only when lightning flashed that they could see anything in the dark night. In the huge waves, they could not see the whitewater of the waves breaking over submerged rocks.

Then, as the sound of waves hitting the shoal intruded, Gunnar had looked at the others and said, "It's been a pleasure serving with you, mates." His was the last human voice Tor had heard.

Now, he took stock in what he had. It was not much. His blue wool tunic had been reduced to rags covering parts of his torso and upper arms. Below the elbows, it was worn away completely. The color was faded to dull white with the faintest blue tint and darker blue near the underarm area. His black trousers were faded to dull gray with lighter streaks. Ragged strips of cloth hung below the torn knees. His woolen socks and cowhide boots were long gone. He still had his small neck knife in the little sheath that hung on a silver chain around his neck. The blade was only three knuckles long and would be of little use in his current situation. He had had no time to gather his shoulder bag that held a fire striker, some fishing line, and a dagger. He would miss those items. He had nothing in which to catch rainwater, except his mouth.

His physical assessment was just as demoralizing. He had no food and no way to catch fish. He had no way to protect his eyes or face from the sun. His clothes offered little protection from the blazing spring sun and none from the cold. His stomach was knotted in hunger pangs, his throat dry. His mouth was sore from scurvy, with no hope of fresh greens. He decided he would probably go crazy from thirst and start drinking seawater, which he knew would kill him before hunger. His muscles were weak from malnutrition, and he knew his end was near.

In his despair, he tried to cry, but he could not muster the energy—or the tears, for that matter. He thought of his family, all dead, and his depression worsened.

CHAPTER 4
THE WILL TO SURVIVE

T he waters had calmed to the point where Tor could carefully sit up on his drifting board without tipping over. Looking in all directions, he saw only water. The waves were gently rolling, less than waist high to him, he reckoned. There were no features that indicated there was land in any direction. That southeast storm was rebuilding and had advanced to the northeast and was now closer as it wrapped around toward the west. His only hint at directions came from the sun overhead and the memory of it rising over those clouds earlier.

Tor spotted something just breaking the water's surface several ells away. He lay down and began paddling toward the odd-shaped object, hoping it might be something from the *Sea Ox*.

When he got to it, he discovered it was floating seaweed. He knew that in some places, they ate the stuff like cabbage. He went to pick a piece off and discovered it was rotten and slimy. The bit he pulled off released a noxious, gassy odor that would have made him sick if he had anything in his stomach. He used what strength he had left to paddle away from the sulfurous smell.

Soon he found himself amid more seaweed. Looking around, he saw a greenish stem that resembled a plant. He picked it up to discover it was long, and its stem disappeared deep under the surface. This was a still-living plant.

He wrestled a portion onto his board, removed his neck knife and cut off a piece. He tried a small bite. His teeth and gums were so sore, it was difficult to bite and chew. The stuff was salty, but it did taste something like cabbage. He was so hungry, he thought about eating it all but decided he should not. He managed to get down a mouthful, then waited to see how his stomach reacted. In a short time, when he did not get sick, he found himself craving more.

So, he ate. And then ate some more. He found that the outer part of the plant stem was very salty, but inside tasted like fresh water. Soon enough, his stomach ached from eating so much too quickly. And not long after that, his stomach revolted and emptied itself. He heaved every morsel he had swallowed, leaving his throat sore and his mouth sour with no way to rinse it out. Once again, he was hungry and weak, feeling helpless.

As the sun worked its way toward the western horizon, he could see lightning flashing in the northeast. He knew he needed to force down more of the green seaweed. He would need every bit of energy he could glean from it. This time, he stopped himself after a few small bites.

When night descended, Tor felt a little stronger. He could now distinctly make out streaks of lightning across the darkening sky far to the east, and he could hear the first faint rumblings of thunder.

Soon the storm was upon him. The east wind gained strength, and the waves began to grow, propelling him once more toward the west.

The storm quickly grew to gale-force winds, continuous thunder, lightning, and slashing rain. In no time, his thirst was quenched, and his skin was cold from the pounding rain drops. He could only hang onto his board desperately as the storm raged. Soon the waves were the size of great halls as they carried him into the unknown.

Frightened to his core, he began to cry again. His despair was so great, he almost deliberately rolled into the thrashing sea to end his misery.

Then Tor heard his grandfather's calming voice as he recalled the day his puppy had been killed when she spooked a cow and was kicked in the head by the big animal. Tor had wailed uncontrollably in his mother's arms for a spell when Papa tore him from her arms and took him for a walk.

"You'll put no soul back in that pup's body by carrying on like this, boy," the elder had said. Tor worshipped his Papa, so he listened. "Bad things happen in life, son," the elder continued. "A man takes each crisis as it comes. He uses his head"— he tapped Tor on his small head—"he grieves his loss, then he picks up the pieces and moves on. You will find that pups, cows, horses, even people will come into your life, be part of it. But they all hold a precious thread of life that can be broken in an instant. We have little control over who, or what, in our lives will perish when we are least prepared. But we, the living, must carry on. God teaches us that. Do you follow what I say, young Tor?"

Sobbing at the memory, Tor replied to the voice, "Yes, Grandfather, I hear you." Tor vowed he would cry no more and would find a way to survive until someone found him in the middle of this great sea. The storm raged on around him.

CHAPTER 5
A GOOD DAY

Tor lost track of how long the storm lasted, but he was physically spent when the wind slacked, and the seas began to quiet. Exhausted, he had no idea if it was day or night when he drifted into a dreamless sleep.

He gained consciousness somewhere around midday. Looking around, he found he was surrounded by a plain of greenish-brown seaweed. He picked some and slowly, carefully ate. This time, he quickly felt stronger. He may have found a way to stay alive, but for how long?

As the afternoon wore on, he found himself dipping into the water to cool his hot skin. The water was quite warm, but not hot like the air. After a while, he found that he had drifted out of the seaweed, not even sure of what direction he was moving. For the first time in recent memory, he was not hungry.

In a flash, he noted a small fish as it darted past him. Then another, and another. Soon, the surface was alive with the hand-sized, slender fish. He recognized them as herring. *If I only had a way to catch some. I could eat them raw!*

A movement caught Tor's peripheral vision. He looked to his right and saw a dolphin's fin. More dolphins appeared until soon he was surrounded by many fast-moving dolphins. The herring were doing everything they could to escape the hungry predators.

Suddenly a herring jumped right onto his plank. Tor smothered it with what was left of his tunic. Eventually he had trapped seven or eight of the twenty or so that landed on his board.

The dolphins herded the small fish into a giant ball just below the surface and a little in front of Tor. They attacked the ball containing thousands of herring until only a few were remaining. Pieces of dead herring littered the water's surface.

After the massacre, the dolphins seemed to play around the area until the sun was setting in the west. Several of the animals took an interest in him, surfacing right alongside his little raft like they were studying him. When one came close and swam at his side he reached out and ran his hand down the animal's back. The creature seemed to like it and stayed for a time. Then another bullied in to get its back rubbed. Tor was fascinated. When the sun began to set, they all seemed to disappear.

Tor wondered if he was the first Norseman to ever pet a dolphin.

CHAPTER 6
NIGHTMARES

After consuming three of the now dead herring, Tor lay back and looked up into the heavens. The night sky was a blanket of stars. Tor could not recall them ever looking so bright. After careful study, he was able to recognize a few clusters. They were in slightly different positions than his father and the other sailors had taught him. Eventually, he found the North Star, discovering he was far, far west of Iceland and much farther south than he could imagine. *How could I have moved so far?*

Sleep finally overtook him, *and he dreamed of catching fish in his stream back on the farm in Ulfr-land. When he lay back to sleep in the soft grass, his thoughts drifted to his favorite scene.*

Tor looked down into the Ulfrfjord valley. He noted

his father's great hall and below it, the shipworks. Bjarni, Einar, Gunnar, and Gorm were building a coastal fishing vessel.

A movement out on the fjord caught his attention. It was a dragon! No...two. They had large, billowing black and white sails with a snarling wolf's head painted on them. They bore toward the shipworks. Then, he saw many of the warships farther down the fjord. There must have been eighty of them.

He tried to run down to warn Father, but his feet and legs were mired, and he could not move. They would never hear his shouts. He could do nothing but look on in horror.

The first two ships beached at the shipworks. Warriors in black armor stormed over the ships' sides and attacked the crew building the fishing vessel. The four unarmed men were helpless against the raiders and soon lay headless in pools of red.

The warriors destroyed the small boat, then set fire to the smithy before charging up the hill toward the hall. Father, Mother, Gerna, Sven, Unndis holding her little babe, Caomh, Cinnia, and their little girl all came out of the hall in white sleeping clothes. Only Father carried a sword.

Some of the raiders went straight to the barn and pens, where they started slaughtering animals including Gerna's pony.

Gerna broke Mother's grasp and ran toward the

dying beast as it thrashed in the pen with two spears protruding from bloody wounds. An arrow struck her in the back and thrust out from her chest. Her white gown turned red as she fell to the ground.

Father fought valiantly, downing two of the warriors. But they got back up and resumed the attack. An ax finally cleaved Father's chest, turning his shirt red as he dropped. Sven fell in a similar fashion, as did Caomh.

By this time, a brute had Mother on the ground, raping her. Two others had Unndis and Cinnia in a similar way. A line of men stood by, waiting their turn.

Another group came out of the now smoking hall with all manner of treasure and possessions. In seconds, the hall was ablaze.

To the east, the entire village was a roaring inferno. The church bell tower flames grew nearly as high as the hill where Tor stood helplessly watching his whole world go up in flames. Even Lokhilla's hall east of the village was on fire.

Warriors ran from the village carrying goods and several kicking young women and girls.

Looking back, Tor saw that many men had finished raping Mother, Unndis, and Cinnia. All three lay with bloody legs spread and long spears through their chests.

Tor awoke, bolting to a sitting position, nearly capsizing his plank. He was shaking and drenched in cold sweat. Images of the dream began to fade.

He looked up and saw a half moon hanging just over the western horizon. He could not remember seeing it rise in the east the previous night.

Tor looked around as the light of dawn began to brighten the eastern sky. What he saw, less than two hundred *stikke* to the south, shot abject fear into his soul. It was the fin of a huge shark fin gliding to the east. He had never dreamed they grew so monstrous. The shark circled him, and when it reached his north side, just as the sun was popping up, Tor could see the size of the deadly predator just below the surface. It was at least twice the length of his plank. He began to shake uncontrollably.

I have no way to escape, and this board has no protection.

Tor was certain his life would end on the jagged teeth inside that huge creature's mouth. He watched the thing circle all the way around him. The monster surfaced as it came along the south side, less than ten stikke away, and looked him in the eye. At that moment he knew he would die a horrible death, and no one would ever know.

So what? No one is left who would care anyway, he thought. Tor resigned himself to his destiny and began to pray to God for his soul.

The shark circled to about sixty ells behind Tor's plank and started in a straight line for his rear. It occurred to Tor that the big spikes were still sticking out the bottom of the deck board. If he could move quickly toward the front just as the shark started to bite, the nails might injure the creature enough to scare it off.

Tor watched the big mouth open as it approached. The creature looked as if it could swallow him in one gulp, plank and all. The young man froze, paralyzed with fear.

The monster was still a few paces back when Tor heard a dull thump. The shark twisted, then another thump. The animal jerked away, blood streaming from its gill slits. It jerked again as another thump could be heard.

Then Tor watched as several dolphin fins broke the surface all around the floundering shark. The smaller dolphins continued to ram into the big animal's belly. Before long, the lifeless body of the shark sank under the water. The dolphins seemed to celebrate even more raucously than they did after feasting on the herring the night before.

Tor earnestly thanked them as two of the friendly dolphins swam up to him to get their backs rubbed. He fed them the four herring he had left, for which they seemed grateful based on the way they played, splashed, and chattered around him.

Tor spent the rest of the day contemplating

what he had witnessed. He wondered where the dolphins had gone at night and what had brought them back just as the shark was about to attack him. He replayed the scene over and over in his head, trying to make sense of what had happened as the adrenaline slowly leached out of his bloodstream.

It was late afternoon when he came back to the present. He saw he was back in the seaweed and filled his empty stomach again. He realized it no longer hurt his mouth to chew the stuff, and he managed to keep down larger quantities.

When Tor's stomach was full, he looked around in the fading light and saw lightning off to the northeast. "Well, at least I'm alive, and my belly is full," he said, just to hear his own voice.

When the sun was setting, he noted that it seemed to disappear before it was swallowed by the sea. *Wonderful, storms coming from both sides,* he smiled in resignation.

CHAPTER 7
LANDFALL

T or slid off the plank and released his evening water in what was left of his trousers. He then splashed and kicked around to wash the urine out of the thin cloth and off his skin before climbing back onto the board. In the faintest light, he thought he saw three large birds skimming just above the water toward the north, far to the west. As the darkness surrounded him, he wondered if he had really seen anything or if his imagination was playing tricks on him.

He did not have long to ponder the question, as the east wind began to pick up and the waves grew larger and more erratic. Thunder rumbled loudly and lightning began to flash in the darkening sky. "Here we go again," he murmured.

The night wore on, waves growing larger and

more powerful. The winds were fierce, lightning close and bright, thunder loud and constant. He grew weary clinging to the board but knew he had to hang on. Night passed into day and back into night with little discernible change in the light reaching his exhausted eyes. Tor had no idea how long the storm tossed him across the sea like a leaf on bare ground in autumn. The only good news was that he was able to quench his thirst with the pouring rain.

One night—he did not know when, for he had lost count—Tor heard a roaring sound. *What is that sound? Could it be another shoal?* Only then did Tor realize the thunder had faded, moving off to the west.

The waves began to slacken, and he worked onto his back to try to catch more rain in his mouth. It had diminished to a soft shower.

Then the waves grew and moved faster, the roaring louder. Tor rolled back onto his belly as he felt the board surge forward. The waves were breaking just in front of him now. He gripped the board for all he was worth. Suddenly he was riding up in front of a growing wave and moving faster than ever. The wave broke, driving him under the water. He clung to the board. It hit the ocean bottom hard, jarring him, but still he clung to the plank. He held his breath as he was rolled over and dragged across coarse, gravelly sand. He felt the shreds of clothes rip off his back.

In a heartbeat, he surfaced and was back on top of the board and being propelled on another wave. Again, he was driven into the sand on the shoal. This time he was flipped off the board, though Tor managed to hang on desperately with one hand. The fronts of his legs bore the punishment of the coarse sand. He never noticed he was completely naked. He found himself in deeper water again. Even though the waves were still rough, they were no longer breaking on the shoal.

His breath was ragged as he tried to recover from the exertion of clinging to the plank while it was violently driven by the powerful waves. Time passed as he was carried along by the rolling waves.

Wait...am I turned around? I hear another shoal in front as the one behind has faded from my hearing. No, the one in front is no shoal—it is a beach! Tor could hear the waves crashing on hard-packed sand.

Without warning, the waves became bigger and faster. The sound of the waves crashing on the beach was thunderous and erratic. Suddenly, the board lurched forward. His plank flipped, and he lost contact with it. The wave drove him under the water and pounded him into packed sand. He scrambled to get back to the surface. No sooner did he get a breath of air than another wave crashed down on him, crushing him into the sand again. The process repeated itself several times until he found himself being rolled across hard-packed sand by a wave. Saltwater and sand filled his mouth, and he gagged.

The next wave carried him farther up the beach. He struggled to stand but could only crawl. The receding waves dragged him back into deeper water until the next breaker drove him down into the sand and pushed him onto the beach again. The process repeated itself until he was too weak to fight. Somehow a big wave carried him far up the beach and deposited him there. The next few waves barely reached him, then none did. He managed to get onto his hands and knees and crawl up the incline of the beach. The sand became softer about the time his strength gave out.

He rolled onto his back and lay there looking up. There were no stars, only darkness. His whole body hurt like never before. His skin burned from the countless scratches incurred while tumbling in the surf and out on the shoal. Hard rain started again, giving his dry mouth some relief, and cooling his naked, bruised body and scraped skin. He began to tremble uncontrollably. Total exhaustion finally overtook him and, mercifully, sleep came.

CHAPTER 8
FOUND

he sun caressed his cheek, and Tor winced.

Why is it so hot up here in this high meadow? It is always so cool. And the creek is roaring with runoff from the snow melt.

Fishing was out of the question, so he had set his pole aside and laid down to nap. Suddenly, Gerna was yelling somewhere, her voice shrill, using words he could not understand, and his head hurt. His mouth felt like the floor of a horse's stall, as if he had drunk too much mead.

Then his young sister was poking him with a stick. "Gerna, stop poking me! Leave me alone!" Tor yelled, but his voice was just a rasping whisper.

Tor rolled to his side and opened his blurry eyes. Home was gone like steam off a red hot iron plate in the smithy. Before him stood an old man with almost white shoulder-length hair hanging in two braids on either side of his head, behind his ears. He wore a sleeveless leather vest with seashells sewn on it in various patterns. What looked like bird tracks were tattooed on his temples and forehead. A faded black geometric bar tattoo ran from ear to ear and over his huge, hooked nose. His arms were skinny and dark colored with sagging, wrinkled skin. Old, faded tattoos formed rings on his upper arms and designs on his shoulders and chest. The only other clothing he wore was some kind of animal skin held up by a leather thong around his waist, covering his privates. His skinny legs were wrinkled and bare, skin sagging that was once shaped by muscle. Finely tanned animal skins with seashells and bead decorations covered his feet.

The pain of moving jolted Tor—he hurt from head to toe. The old man poked him in the ribs with the stick.

How long have I been here? Tor wondered. *Every part of my body hurts, especially my skin. It feels like I am on fire. And the sun is hot. No wait...it is just above the horizon. I have scrapes all over my body. How? Oh, the waves crushed me into the sand and gravel. The beach is almost dry. It was wet and raining, I think.*

He struggled to a sitting position and rested his weary head on arms crossed over bent knees.

The part of his body that had lain exposed to the sun was burning up. The rest just burned from the scrapes. The old man poked him in the ribs again. Tor tried to look at the man, but everything was blurry. He looked and was startled when he saw two older boys stationed on either side of him, each with a short stick in their hands. Tied to those sticks were what looked like pig shoulder blades that had been sharpened to a point. They looked ready to use them on him.

Through gritty, blurry eyes, Tor noticed the boy closest to him had what looked like a water bag hanging at his side. Tor feebly pointed to the bag. When he raised his arm, the boy drew his stick up like he would strike him. Tor dropped his arm, but then pointed to his mouth. The boy questioningly cocked his head. Tor pointed to the bag again with a shaky hand and then to his mouth. He tried to say "water", but it came out as just a hoarse, slurred sound. The boy caught on and started to lift the bag off his shoulder when the old man said something to stop him.

The boy said something back that sounded like he was pleading with the old man. The old man said something to the other boy, who responded by raising his stick over Tor's head. The first boy carefully handed the water skin to Tor, but his arms and hands were shaking so badly he could not hold it up. The boy looked at the old man, then put the opening to Tor's mouth and lifted it. In his short life, Tor had never felt anything so wonderful as that tepid water flowing into his mouth. He did not care what it tasted like. He had no idea how long it had been since he tasted the rain while he lay on the beach in a storm, but he knew this was life. The boy pulled the skin away before Tor was ready to stop but he was thankful and nodded to the boy who he could now see was, perhaps, a little older than himself.

The old man prodded him in the ribs with that stick again, motioning for him to stand up. Tor could see it was an ornately carved and painted walking stick. Alas, he felt too weak to stand. After several more jabs from the stick, Tor rolled over onto his knees. The sand bit into the scrapes on his legs, and he knew he had to get up—it hurt too much to stay in that position. As he brought one knee forward, the two older boys brought their sticks into a ready position. He feared that if he had any water in him, he would start crying. It took all his leg strength, plus both hands braced on his knee, but he managed to stagger to his feet. He stood there wobbling on shaky legs and weak knees, but at least he was standing. His head was spinning, and he felt dizzy.

One of the boys moved in front of him, and the

other stayed at his side as the old man told them something. Next, the old man stepped behind him and two little children, a boy, and a girl, fell in behind the old man. They were silent the whole time and looked at him with fear in their eyes. They looked about Gerna's age. They were both naked from head to toe, like him. *God in heaven, Gerna is dead!* It hit Tor like a punch to the gut. He gave them a sad smile and turned back to the old man, who motioned him to look ahead.

The boy in front beckoned him to follow as he walked up the beach toward the tall grasses that grew in patches among the sand dunes above the beach. As he glanced to his right, it seemed as if the beach went on forever in a straight line. To his left, it stretched at least a half a league before it curved out of sight. Before the beach curved to the west, he noticed an opening where a small river flowed into the sea. Slowly, he stumbled behind the boy leading him up the rise of the dunes. As they approached, a trail emerged through the grasses, leading the way to the top. After they topped the first dune, the small hill leveled out for about a hundred paces before rising a little, then dropping off.

As they got to the crest, Tor could see there was a body of water on the other side of the dunes with land beyond that. On the far side, mud and grasses gave way to scattered small trees, then thickets and, finally, forest. The channel had exposed mudflats on both sides dotted with rushes and tall grasses. The smell of rotting vegetation filled the air. He presumed the tide was out.

When their group began descending from the dunes, several large birds that looked like some sort of herons awkwardly took flight, squawking their displeasure at the intrusion. Some were white, some were gray. A long, hollowed-out log sat at the edge of a small channel that led through the mudflat to the open water of the big channel. The channel stretched north as far as Tor could see.

The boy in front went to the far end of the log and pulled it into the small channel. The second boy followed to help manage the heavy log. The old man poked him in the back and motioned for him to get in. Tor had never seen such a thing. It did not look safe to climb over the side, and it sure did not look seaworthy enough to carry their whole party out into that channel. But the old man kept poking him with that stick, so he had to try.

Next came the problem of where to climb in. Right in the center, there was a raised, flat, round place. It looked sort of like a seat, but the flat part was charred as if small fires had burned there at times in the past. Other than that, there were raised spots close to both ends where the boys were holding the log against the small muddy channel. The boy behind him, holding the near end, motioned for Tor to get in just in front of the little flat place in the middle.

Tor worked his way up to the side in the knee-deep water and tried to climb in. His arms and legs were too shaky and had no strength. He simply could not do it. He hung his head in despair. Suddenly, the boy closest to him wrapped his arms around Tor from behind, lifted him over the side and plopped his butt down into the hollowed log. The whole thing felt wobbly, and Tor expected it to tip over at any moment.

The little children slogged through the water alongside the log and when they got to their places, slithered over the side like a couple of serpents. The log hardly even wiggled. Next, the old man climbed in with the help of the boy at the far end. The boy who had helped the old man followed next, jumping in with a graceful hop, and took up a paddle that lay on the floor. Finally, the boy at the rear end of the log shoved it into the deeper water, then hopped in himself and took up the other paddle. The boys back paddled the log into the open channel, then turned and paddled south, parallel to the shoreline.

Tor was amazed at how quickly these two boys

were moving this unseemly boat through the water. He was still afraid it would sink or capsize. After a short time, they came to the small river that cut through the island on the ocean side and emptied out of the forested land to the west. They turned upstream and headed into the forest.

Some distance upstream they rounded a bend and saw a large clearing ahead on the right. In the clearing stood a solid wall of poles lashed together in what looked like a large oval or circle. Trails of wood smoke rose from several places beyond the wall of poles which were about three times the height of a man. About every thirty paces were bastions where lookouts or archers could stand guard, protecting what was behind the wall. No one was visible to him in any of those bastions.

Outside the wall, scattered around a field and into the forest, there were hundreds of conical-shaped tents. Many had cooking fires tended by shirtless women. Countless naked and half-dressed children were shouting and running all over the place, chasing dogs, sticks, round hoops, and each other. Pulled up on a flat beach several paces below the pole wall were what looked like more than three hundred hollowed-out logs like the one he was in.

A shout rose among the people milling around outside the pole wall as the boys paddled their log toward the beach. Tor noted that all the people were of that dark, tanned color. Suddenly, more shouts rang out, and people started moving en masse toward the river. A stream of people from within the walled enclosure came running out. Tor realized that the ends of the wall overlapped, leaving a gap where people could enter or leave.

The rush of people made Tor's stomach queasy, like it had been when the shark was about to attack him. As his log slid to a stop, he noticed an old woman waddle out of the pole enclosure, hobbling along with the aid of a stick much like the one used by the old man.

She was dressed in a finely-tanned-animal-skin sleeveless dress decorated with shells, beads, and ink designs. Her white hair was gathered in a tight bun on her head and pinned with bone and copper hair pins. Around her neck was a string-like necklace with a decorated shell hanging on it, along with several bead and shell necklaces that hung in different lengths down her front. Her wrists bore copper and shell bead bracelets. She had tattoos on her cheeks, forehead, and temples, though Tor was too far away to see what the tattoos depicted. The old woman raised her hand, and the gathered crowd fell silent.

The two little children were first out of the hollowed-out log. They splashed through the water and sprinted up the bank to join a younger woman who had moved next to the old woman. The children wrapped their arms around the woman's legs and slid behind her. She was dressed in an animal skin skirt painted with walking, long-necked birds around the hem. Below the hem, the skirt was fringed. A small, beaded belt was tied around her waist, and a finely tanned red fox skin was draped over one shoulder with the fur out and the tail down her back. The fox skin was attached to the belt by a wide leather thong. It covered one breast and exposed the other, which was decorated with tattoos as well. Her hair fell in a single braid down her back and was tied off with beaded strings. A large reddish feather was pinned high on her head with a small bone pin, letting the feather hang down. She, too, had tattoos on her face. Looking around, Tor noticed that almost all the adults bore tattoos on their faces, shoulders, chests, and arms.

"What is it you have found on the beach, husband?" the old woman asked loudly in a language that Tor did not understand, other than that it was a question.

"I wish I knew, *Sakimaxkwe*. It appears to be a boy, but none like I have ever seen or heard of. Perhaps some of our guests can shed light on this mystery," the old man answered in similar gibberish while shrugging his shoulders.

The two boys sprung from the log with grace and helped the old man to his feet and out into the shallow water. He hobbled up the bank using his stick to steady his thin legs. With an unseen gesture, the boy in front summoned two other young men to help lift Tor out of the log. They approached cautiously with vicious-looking clubs in their hands and scowls on their faces. The boy from the canoe said something, and the young men reattached their clubs to their waist belts. Each wore only a piece of animal skin tied with a leather thong around his waist. Both had those bird tracks tattoos on their temples and foreheads.

They grabbed Tor roughly under the arms and lifted him out of the log boat. His legs were still unsteady. He was weak from lack of food and desperately thirsty. The young men shoved him toward the crowd that had gathered at the top of the riverbank. He plodded one unsteady step at a time. He tried not to show the fear that consumed him, but he was quite sure his face betrayed him. The fact he was stark naked did not add to his comfort, but he had no control over the situation so he ignored the problem as best he could. Finally, he reached the flat and stood in front of the old woman.

She was flanked by the old man and the younger woman with the two children. A fierce-looking man stood next to and slightly in front of the younger woman. He had several bear-track tattoos on his cheeks and forehead and a wolf track tattoo on each temple, along with a geometric design. A large bear was tattooed on his chest. His hair was a single roach hanging from the back, right side of his head. It was braided and fell down his back. The skin wrapped around his waist hung down the front halfway to his knees and was fringed and decorated with beads and quills.

The old woman produced a string of sounds that may have been words. It sounded as if she was asking Tor a question.

All he could do was stare at her. Tor did not understand anything she was saying, or even if they were words or some magical spell. He felt dizzy, and everything became blurry as Tor's world began to spin out of control before going black.

CHAPTER 9

A NEW LIFE

W hen he awoke, Tor was lying on a skin on the ground with another covering him. His head was against the pole wall, and he was in the shade of an overhanging thatched roof. He was warm but weak. Seated next to him was the boy from the log boat who had sat behind him. When Tor opened his eyes, the boy spoke to someone who then ran off. He looked around and saw a throng of people in a big semicircle, staring at him while keeping their distance. They were mumbling among themselves, but Tor had no inkling of what they were saying. He noted the boy now wore bright yellow paint on his chest, back, arms, and legs.

A short time later, a younger boy arrived with a cup made from a hollowed-out piece of wood. It was tea of some kind that tasted good although a little bitter. Tor recognized a mint flavoring and something sweet. It felt good going down, but his stomach roiled. He barely managed to keep it down. Next, the younger boy reached into a pouch that hung over his shoulder and pulled out a piece of dried meat. It looked like beef and tasted divine as Tor bit off a chunk, chewed it as quickly as he could, and swallowed. Again, his stomach rebelled, and he realized he had to slow down. He could not make up for weeks of starvation in one meal. He wiped his mouth and discovered for the first time how blistered and swollen his lips were. *No wonder people are staring at me*, he thought. *I must look horrible.*

The young man beside him looked at him, pointed to himself and said something. To Tor, it was just sound. He tried to say his own name, but his voice came out as only a hoarse squeak. The boy looked at him again, pointed to himself saying, "*Chitaninu Lunkon*, Strong Wing." Tor thought about it and realized the boy was saying his name. He remembered how his father had told him about communicating with the Skræling, Peluk—that learning each other's names was an important first step. He tried to imitate the boy's words, but they came out all wrong. His tongue was still not very coordinated. He took another drink of tea. It tasted better and felt better in his stomach. He tried again. Strong Wing repeated over and over until Tor could consistently reiterate Strong Wing's name. Both felt a sense of accomplishment.

Tor pointed to himself and slowly said, "Tor." Strong Wing looked at him and cocked his head. The younger boy just returned with more tea, which Tor eagerly drank. He tried to pronounce his name as simply and clearly as possible. Finally, Strong Wing said, "Tuh," and both boys nodded their heads and smiled.

About that time, the fierce-looking man came up and said something to Strong Wing. *It sounded like Strong Wing was in some sort of trouble. Maybe he was supposed to make sure I died!* Strong Wing looked apologetically at Tor, picked up his bag, and disappeared behind the pole wall.

Tor pulled himself up to a sitting position and looked up at the man, who was menacingly scowling at him. He began to realize his whole body was covered with some sort of fat. He could smell a mint fragrance and something else he could not identify, but his skin did not burn as badly as it had earlier. He also noticed he was wearing one of those skins covering his private areas, tied around his waist with a leather thong.

They must want to keep me alive!

He was surprised to see so many people

around. From what he had heard, there were not this many Skræling in all of Vinland, which is where he assumed he was. As soon as he could communicate, they would put him in contact with the Greenlanders, and he would get to Uncle Thorkell's farm before summer was over.

Tor pointed to himself, smiled, and said "Tor" as plainly as he could. The man just shook his head. Tor repeated his name again and again. At last, the man caught on and said, "Tuh" in a deep guttural voice. Tor decided these people had no "R" sound in their vocabulary in the same manner as the Norse, so Tor smiled and nodded his head vehemently, thinking that is close enough for now. The man smiled back, pointed to a bear claw that hung on a leather thong around his neck and said, "*Maxkw Hwikash*, Bear Claw," then pointed to himself. It took Tor several tries before he mastered it, but the man looked pleased when he did.

Tor thought he may as well try to get along with these people. *Who can guess how long it will take them to get me to Greenland? I should try to help them, so they will want to help me.*

CHAPTER 10

A GAME

O ut across the field rose a chorus of yelling, cheering, and jeering. Tor could not see, for the crowd stood between him and the field, but when the shouting started, most turned and moved off in that direction. His guardian looked toward the field anxiously, then down at him. He beckoned Tor to stand. Feeling somewhat stronger, he found he could accomplish the task fairly quickly. Bear Claw then indicated they should move toward the noise.

Tor hobbled along as fast as his sore, weak legs could carry him until they stood at the edge of a marked part of the field. The grass in the marked area was beat down shorter than the surrounding grass, as if it had been trampled for days. It was dry but had been muddy with heavy traffic. The marked area was about fifty paces long and thirty paces wide. The people opened a wide swath for them to pass. When they did, Tor could see what was happening.

Some sort of a contest was being held in the marked section of the large field. People crowded the sides while a group of young men or boys formed on one side of the middle line and a group of young women or girls formed on the other side of a line down the middle of the marked area. The men and women wore only loincloths and were decorated with bright paint on their arms, chests, backs, and legs. The men all wore yellow paint while the women wore blue. Their hair was worn loose, and some wore feathers twined into their flowing black hair. A few of the men had shaved their heads except for a roach on the back, right side, like the man standing next to him.

On both ends of the marked area were two posts about four to five paces apart that stood tall above the center of the end line. Two elders stood on the side of the marked area and near the center-line. At their feet lay a pile of several straight sticks about an ell long. Another elder carried a ball made of an animal skin and stuffed with something to make it stay round. Tor guessed the ball to be about the size of an average human head. The elder carried the ball to the center of the line and raised it above his head with much flourish and showmanship. The players scattered to favored locations. On a signal, the elder tossed the ball straight up, and the players went after it.

Tor quickly noticed that the men's team could only kick the ball to pass it from one to another before trying to kick it between the posts on their side of the field. The women could pick up the ball and run with it, throw it, or kick it to one another to move it toward their goal. The ball went back and forth for some time. Tor noted that the women could grab or tackle the men, while the men were allowed only to steal the ball from the women. A couple of times, a man kicked the ball toward their posts and missed. The women then would be given the ball and start moving it back toward the other end. The crowd was yelling frantically for one side or the other. Bear Claw shouted encouragement to Strong Wing whenever he kicked the ball or stole it from a woman.

In no time, the players were covered with sweat. More than once, a violent collision caused one or more players to be helped off or carried from the playing field. A group of replacement players stood ready to take the place of any injured comrade. Broken and bloody noses were becoming commonplace.

Eventually, a man kicked the ball between the

two posts. The ball was brought back to the center of the field, and the elder representing the men ceremoniously took a stick from his pile and laid it on the ground with a flourish and in a certain place. Next, the elder holding the ball threw it up again, and the game restarted.

As the game wore on, both sides scored and the sticks were lined up in rows, one for the men and one for the women. Tor found his legs becoming too weak to stand and sat cross-legged on the edge of the playing field. Bear Claw was so enthralled with the game, he did not even notice. In a short while, a young girl came along and offered Bear Claw a few cakes of some kind. He made sure Tor got a couple of them, too. They were flavored with blackberries and honey. Tor was grateful for the nourishment, and soon he felt strong enough to stand up again.

Finally, Strong Wing kicked the ball between the poles on the men's side and a great cheer went up. Bear Claw turned to Tor and lifted him off the ground, jumping around and yelling something. When they were ready to start the game again, each side had eleven sticks lined up on the ground, and the sun was near the western treetops. The contest had started just after midday, Tor judged by the location of the sun and the experience gained while at sea. The players were exhausted and during the break stood around with their hands on their knees, chests heaving. Tor learned from Bear Claw that the women's team was from another village, and the men were from this village.

Play resumed with a new eagerness. All the players had serious looks on their faces and played their hardest. Tor wished he could be out there. He knew he could not in his present condition but felt he would regain his strength eventually. Both teams came close to getting the ball between the posts but failed. At last, after the sun had set and the light was fading, Strong Wing got the ball with a chance to kick it between the goal posts. His kick was true. A woman dived for the ball and tipped it, but it careened off the post and went through to score the winning point for the home team. Again, Bear Claw lifted Tor up and jumped around yelling with jubilation. During the game, Tor picked up on the words in the Skræling language for man, woman, boy, girl, run, kick, ball, and other terms and phrases associated with the game of *pahsaheman*.

The crowd entered the playing field and hugged the players, squared bets, slapped backs, and generally had a good time before they started moving to another location in the big field where a huge bonfire was just being lit. Someone came up and handed Bear Claw a necklace of dazzling painted shells.

When they found him, Strong Wing was happy to see Tor up and around. He did note that Tor's skin still looked excruciatingly red and painful, but Strong Wing was much too thrilled with his own success in the game to worry about the foreign boy's problems. The young man thought he earned some black drink on this day and was looking forward to his first taste as a man. He also had a certain young woman on his mind.

CHAPTER II
GAINING STRENGTH

Activities at the bonfire and the adjoining dance plaza struck Tor as being similar in nature to some of the feasts he had witnessed back home in Haakon's great hall when the men returned from some of their more successful raids. The adults enjoyed drinks forbidden to children and participated in all sorts of wild activities for days and nights at a time. The raucous events were a time when Christian order broke down completely. Men ran off to secret locations with other men's wives or unwed widows, maidens, even thralls. Many young men and boys not much older than Tor had their first intimate encounters with the opposite sex. At every one of those homecomings, children were pretty much forgotten and left to fend for themselves. There had been plenty of food and many other children to play with, but there was little adult supervision.

It was no different here, except that the dances were much more organized. The music was produced on big drums and flutes rather than stringed instruments and by poets. Here, the dancers were organized into some form of groups he did not understand, and they went on for hours, jumping and weaving, stomping, depicting wild animals and visitors from some spirit worlds. Many chanted while they danced. As the night wore on, Tor became overcome with fatigue and slept through much of it.

One of the children shook him awake at some point and motioned for him to follow, which he did. The boy led him into the pole wall fortress and to a small hall, though it was one of the bigger houses in the village. He was too tired to pay much attention to how things were laid out. Besides, it was dark and hard to see much.

The boy led him into a large room just inside the door, which consisted of an animal skin hanging on a stick at the top of the door opening. He could tell that most of the men would have to duck through the opening, though it was high enough for him to walk through. The old woman who had spoken to him when they arrived stood over by a large fire pit in the center of the room.

She was talking to some young women, pointing to different pots and bags next to the fire. When Tor and the boy entered, she looked up. Her expression toward him was not a very welcoming one. As she seemed to be someone of great importance, Tor would do what he could to get on her good side. Right now, that did not look like it would be easy.

She spoke for a few moments to the boy who had led Tor into the hall, then turned and went through a finely tanned animal skin into another room. The oldest of the women by the firepit, who wore only a brown fabric skirt, followed her.

The boy grabbed a rolled-up animal skin from the outer wall and laid it out on the floor matting in a place that seemed to be out of the way. He motioned for Tor to lie on it, grabbed another skin, and gave it to him to use as a cover. After the walk, and given the late hour, Tor was ready to lay back down. His mind was just drifting into sleep when he heard voices. The old man who had poked him on the beach, Bear Claw, and the woman he took to be Bear Claw's wife came into the room. The old man talked incessantly to no one in particular and walked even more wobbly than Tor remembered. The old man wobbled his way through the door hanging into the back room where the old woman had disappeared. Soon her raised voice could be heard, probably scolding the old man.

Bear Claw and the woman seemed to be talking at each other, jabbing a pointed finger into the other's chest. He heard each mention Strong Wing's name more than once. Finally, they settled onto a sleeping bench along the wall opposite Tor. He could still hear the drums when he was overcome by sleep.

CHAPTER 12
LEARNING

Tor woke to increased activity. The plainly dressed young women, aided by one somewhat older, were tending to things around the fire pit. The little children from the beach were chasing each other back and forth on the other side of the firepit. One or both would look at him every few seconds. When they determined that he was awake, they made sure everyone knew it.

Bear Claw was gone, but the woman he had slept with climbed sleepily out from under her sleeping skin. She had on a light fabric dress that came about halfway down her thighs. He wondered when she had put that on. She was wearing her dance skirt when she slid into the blankets with Bear Claw a few hours earlier. The old woman sat on a raised log platform at the head of the fire pit and talked quietly to the woman who was overseeing things around the fire.

Bear Claw's wife, Red Feather, ran her fingers through her long black hair, put on a pair of skin shoes and ducked out the door. The naked children followed her.

The boy who had brought him there sometime in the night rose from a sleeping skin, came over and motioned Tor to follow him. Tor pointed to his chest and said "Tor." The boy nodded and smiled. Tor pointed to him and opened his hands like a question. "*Ehes,*" the boy said. Tor repeated it, nodded, and smiled. The boy led him out the door and around the back side of the house where he showed Tor the trench to drain his morning water. Tor was happy to go. He could not remember the last time he made water.

As he was finishing and reattaching his loin-cloth, Red Feather came out from behind some shrubs, her children in tow. The children stayed on her side opposite Tor as she walked by, not making eye contact.

Ehes led Tor back toward the other end of the house and stopped by a huge pile of clam, oyster, and other marine shells. He picked up a clamshell, pointed to it and said "*ehes*." Then he pointed to himself and said "Ehes."

Tor smiled, picked up a clamshell, pointed to it and said "ehes," then pointed to the boy and said "Ehes."

Clam Shell nodded and gave Tor a big smile, pointed to Tor and said "Tuh." Tor smiled and nodded happily.

When they went back in the house, the boy led Tor over to where the old woman was licking the last drips of a grayish, yellow-colored gruel from her fingers. She handed the bowl to one of the girls as they walked up to her. Clam Shell excitedly said, "Grandmother, this boy has a name. It is 'Tuh!'" The only word that Tor understood was his name.

"Yes, I know, your father already told me," the old woman replied coldly. He hung his head and started to walk away when she added, "But it is good that you have talked to him. Maybe you can get him to talk about his homeland and how he came to be on our shore? I want you to spend the day with him. Find out what you can. But do not get far away from someone who can help you if this Tuh turns against you. Understand?"

Tor understood none of what she said.

Clam Shell nodded and led Tor to an empty area next to the fire pit. Two of the girls immediately brought them each a bowl of gruel and a cup of sassafras tea. Tor did not know what the lumpy, grayish-yellow gruel was, but he liked it when he tasted it.

Just as they were finishing their meal, Strong Wing came slinking into the room. His body paint was smeared, especially on his front side, and smeared handprints could be seen on his back. His hair was unkempt and contained a few pieces of leaves. He had blue paint smeared on his cheeks, chest, and belly. He did not make eye contact with anyone. He just went to his sleeping platform, got something from a bag under it, then started to head back toward the door hanging.

About that time, the old man came into the big room from his chambers in the rear. He looked over Strong Wing and said "So, that Sun Town girl who scored as many times as you, plays other games as well? He-he!" Long Beard was proud of himself for embarrassing Strong Wing. Strong Wing just slapped his thigh with his fist, grunted, and ducked out the door. Everyone except Tor knew he was going to the river. Long Beard took his seat to the right of the old woman and looked around at everyone staring at him. "What?" he said.

"You were young and in his moccasins once,

old man. How did you like being teased by your elders?" Wattle asked sarcastically.

"When one is young and does foolish things, one must pay a price," he snickered.

"Well, some never learn and must pay even as they grow old." Her eyes bore into his.

"Can an old man not get any food around here?" he asked, changing the subject. A girl promptly handed him a bowl of gruel and set a cup of tea on the mat by his seat.

"So, how did our strange guest enjoy his first night in Willet Village?" The old man's eyes landed on Tor, who was desperately trying to pick up a word he might know.

"Our 'guest' has a name, and if you would pay half a lick of attention to anyone but yourself, you would know it already!" Wattle growled at him.

"I think everyone is tired from the dancing last night. We are all irritable. After everyone packs out today, maybe we can get some rest and then try to figure out how to get this one back to his people," Red Feather nodded toward Tor.

"'His people?' Do you think he has people that we can find? Have you ever laid eyes on anyone who looks anything close to what he looks like?" Wattle asked. "Maybe we could just give him a canoe and let him paddle home. Do not be ridiculous. We need only to decide whether to adopt him, sell him, or make him a slave. When all the guests leave, our Council will discuss it. In the meantime, we will let Clam Shell get what information he can from him. They are about the same age—I think this Tuh will talk to him," Wattle sighed. She noted Tor's ears perked up when he heard her say his name, but the foreign boy shrugged his shoulders like he did not understand the exchange in any form.

Bear Claw ducked under the door hanging, walked across the room, and sat down next to Red Feather. Bright-Eyed Boy and Little Star immediately started climbing on his lap and over his broad shoulders. "Some breakfast, please," he announced. In a few heartbeats, a bowl of gruel and a cup of tea were set in front of him. "All of the clans from Sun Town are packed and ready to leave, although an important young woman from the Great Sakimaxkwe's clan got in quite late. Painted Turtle is not in the best of moods this morning. Crab Village and Oyster Shell are close to ready. Round Track and Spur Villages are having trouble finding all their young adults this morning. I did not think the black drink was mixed that strong."

"I mixed it weak because there were so many first-time adults this time," Wattle answered.

"They probably got carried away lifting skirts," she added.

"Where is Strong Wing? Has he not made it home yet?" Bear Claw inquired, looking at Red Feather.

"He came in, his grandfather embarrassed him, and he left for the river to clean up," Red Feather answered.

"It seems the elder has to probe into other people's affairs," Wattle chided.

"I just wonder if he might know where those young people went last...err...this morning," Bear Claw said to no one in particular.

Just then Strong Wing ducked under the door hanging. He was clean, and his hair was still wet. He avoided eye contact and went straight to sit at his father's right side. He looked across the fire pit at Tor and said, "*Hoo, Tuh*," then added, "Are you feeling stronger today?" knowing Tor would not understand.

"*Hoo*, Strong Wing," Tor answered back, smiling.

"Do you know the whereabouts of any of the missing Round Track and Spur Villagers this morning?" Bear Claw turned to look at Strong Wing.

"No, I was with Willow Branch from Sun Town after the dancing ended," Strong Wing answered honestly. "Are they lost? How many are missing?"

"Four people total, two from each village. They came the farthest and would be least familiar with our lands. If they got over toward the rising sun, they could easily get lost in the tall reeds and swamp waters. We had better put a search party together. Eat up, and we will get going." Bear Claw had a hint of concern in his voice. "One more thing, Sakimaxkwe Wattle, the Great Sakimaxkwe, Painted Turtle wishes to know what you will do with the foreigner." Bear Claw directed his eyes to Wattle.

"I will tell her our Council has not yet decided. We will send a runner as soon as a decision has been made. Too many things are going on with the Solstice Celebration and all. I will let her know we will meet sooner rather than later," Wattle replied, looking at Tor. Tor could only look from face to face, wondering what they were talking about.

———

TOR WAS MESMERIZED by the melodic sounds as these people spoke. *Father had said that Peluk could say things in a talking voice that sounded like a song. These people were no different. So many Norsemen said, "They talk in grunts and animal sounds." But if they talk in animal sounds, it is of the most melodious of forest birds,* he thought.

Bear Claw and Strong Wing put on animal skin leggings, shirts, and thick skin shoes, gathered bows and war clubs, and were out the door. Clam Shell and Tor followed, but they were not joining any search party. They walked out into the plaza by the big fire pit.

CHAPTER 13
A NEW FRIEND

B ear Claw led a party of about twenty young and seasoned warriors out of the pole wall and toward the Round Track and Spur Village campsites. Bear Claw broke off from the group and went to the landing where the Sun Town people were loading. Sun Town was the largest village in the region, therefore the Sakimaxkwe, Great Clan Mother, of all the Lenape River people was seated there among the Turtle People. She was also Head Matron of the Turtle Clan.

Bear Claw addressed the Head Matron reverently. "Great Sakimaxkwe, you have a fine day for traveling. Warm air, light winds, and sunny skies. I wish you a speedy and safe trip to Sun Town."

"Thank you, War Chief Bear Claw. Are you the

official send-off delegate of Willet Village?" she replied rather coldly.

"No, Great Sakimaxkwe. I came by to see if you needed anything. It seems some young folks from Round Track and Spur Villages are lost. I have formed a search party to try to find them. I really must be going if you have no further needs right now. Sakimaxkwe Wattle will be here soon with some corn cakes and pemmican for your journey," he answered, looking at the ground.

"Many of the young people kept late hours. My own granddaughter, Willow Branch, tried to sneak in after the light came into the world this morning. I understand she was with a young man from Willet Village. I hope that he is an honorable person." She was quite aware that she was talking to the young man's father.

"Do you know his name? I will make sure he is punished for any indiscretions he has committed," Bear Claw tried to deflect the accusation.

"I do not believe a name is needed. Just tell his uncle that he should be ready to assume responsibility if any complications should arise," she replied. "Young people will do what they do," she added, looking away.

"Yes, Great Sakimaxkwe. I take my leave now. Sakimaxkwe Wattle will be here shortly." Bear Claw was happy to be walking away from that group. He looked toward the palisade and noted Wattle leading a contingent of people bearing baskets and bags of food for the people of Sun Town. He wondered if there would be consequences to pay for Strong Wing's lust. As he turned his attention toward the Round Track Village campsite, he noticed their matron, Wolf Mother, berating two young warriors.

Upon his arrival at the Round Track camp, he learned that the missing young men had returned, and they had been with the two missing young women from Spur Village. Wolf Mother was not pleased that the young men put them behind schedule in departing for their village. Now she would have to wait until Wattle and Painted Turtle exchanged pleasantries and formal farewells.

——————

CLAM SHELL and Tor followed the chief and Long Beard out of the lodge. The morning was warm, with just a slight breeze. The air was humid but not uncomfortable. A few hazy, white clouds could be seen through the tall trees. The sun had not yet risen above the outer wall of the village. Inside the pole wall, the ground was mostly bare from all the foot traffic. Although it had rained a couple of days previously, the dark-colored clay and loamy soil was packed hard and dry.

By now, many people were gathered in the plaza. There were a few men and women dressed in decorated tunics and dresses, and others in very drab work clothes. Tor thought those must be their thralls, though he had no idea what the relationships were like in the world he found himself in. When Wattle and Long Beard hobbled out using their walking sticks to steady their feeble legs, the drably dressed people picked up clay pots and woven baskets and fell in line behind Wattle, Long Beard, Red Feather, and the other people in the clean, beaded clothes. He noted that most were older people.

CHAPTER 14
FITTING IN

S tarting from the pole wall entrance, Clam
Shell led Tor around the village pointing
out things. Tor understood precious little
of what was being said. The first house seen was
Wattle's Turkey Clan longhouse. Between the
longhouse and the wall were some shrubs, bushes,
and tall grass. Behind those were the holes that
they used for their calls to nature. There also was a
hole that contained broken tools, clay pots, worn-
out clothes, and other refuse. Near those was the
large pile of clam, oyster, mussel, crayfish, and
crab shells. Tor could only guess how many years it
took to accumulate that many shells. He noted it
did not smell good behind the house.

Tor noticed the houses and halls were made by
putting the butt end of poles in the ground in two

rows about thirty hands apart. The length of the rows determined the size of the building. The poles were reinforced with saplings tied in rows parallel to the ground in intervals up the poles. The poles were then bent over and lashed together, forming a curve-shaped top. The curved top was further reinforced with saplings tied to the inside. Once shaped, the whole structure was covered with big slabs of bark fastened to the poles and cross braces with bark ropes. The ends were framed with poles and cross ties, then covered with bark slabs. The bark slabs were fastened in an overlapping manner so that they would shed rain-water. After the whole structure was covered with bark, more poles were lashed to the outside to strengthen the building. A few holes were left along the peak of the domed roofline to ventilate smoke from the wood fires inside. Each of these had a slab of bark that could be placed over the hole during storms.

Just off the south side of the big lodge, there was a small spring-fed stream. A pool of clear water from the spring had some log steps leading to a small shelter beside the longhouse that was rather low to the ground and covered with animal hides. Next to it was a fire pit and some pots for holding water. Two of the pots held cedar leaves and berries, as well as what looked to be mint leaves floating in them. From the spring and pool, the small stream meandered through the village.

Tor noted that all the buildings were built the same, with poles and large bark slabs, obviously from very large trees. There were no window openings. Most had only one door located on the east side, but the bigger ones had a smaller door on the west side as well.

The next house was somewhat smaller. It had two posts set on either side of the door with some sort of scary faces carved on them. One face bore a mean, hateful expression and was painted red. The other looked peaceful, almost happy, and was painted white. Little clay pots with fresh food in them stood at the foot of each post. Tor thought it was funny that the camp dogs avoided this area altogether. As they got close to the door, he picked up a slight rotting odor mixed with burnt cedar. Clam Shell quickly passed by the building.

Next was the tallest house in the village. It was larger than any other and was laid out in a square shape. The entrance was covered with a door made of large slabs of bark lashed together on a frame and to the opening. It had taller posts on each side of the door. One post was topped with a carved turtle, the other, a carved long-necked bird like the ones tattooed on several people's faces or painted on their clothes. Below the bird carving was another carving of that bird, a hawk, a wood-pecker, and a heron. Below the turtle were carvings of a bear, a deer, and a fish. Tor noticed that all the doors to all the houses faced east, even the ones on the east along the pole wall, which he could see now was a large oval, almost round, shape.

Clam Shell untied and pulled back the door covering. Inside the large house, it was so dark that it took a few minutes for Tor's eyes to adjust. It was a huge room with a fire pit running about ten ells long, oriented east–west along the center. East and west of the fire pit were tall posts that went all the way to the domed roof. In the center stood a single, heavier, tall post that also reached the roof. Two large oval-shaped masks painted half red and half black, one facing east and the other west, hung on either side of the post. The expressions on the masks were odd. You could see a grin or a grimace, depending on how you looked at the eyes. The mouths formed a circle, as if saying the letter "O," *just like Father had described some of the carvings he had seen when he was with Peluk.*

Benches ran along the straight parts of the long walls. On the posts supporting the outside walls hung many masks depicting animals, spirits, and things Tor could not understand. Under the benches, there were baskets filled with feathers, small turtle-shell rattles, and other objects that Tor supposed were used in various ceremonies. Tor thought this hall must be like a church.

Toward the rear of the building was a partition. In the middle was a door with a skin hanging over it, so he could not see what was back there. Between that partition and the west post was a raised platform that looked big enough to hold sixteen to twenty people. Clam Shell said a little prayer to the mask on the east side of the center post without looking at it and signaled to Tor it was time to leave.

Once outside, their eyes had to readjust to the bright light. In the open plaza, children were playing with dogs, chasing one another, and carrying hoops and sticks. He noticed some were playing a game where one would roll a hoop across the ground while others tried to throw their stick through the rolling hoop. Success was met with whoops and congratulatory slaps on the back.

Next to the longhouses, women lifted short, heavy logs and dropped them into larger diameter hollowed-out stumps, making a deep, thumping sound. Tor looked in one of the hollow stumps and saw that the woman was crushing large, yellow seeds. He realized they were making flour. He had never seen seeds like that before, so he picked up a stray one and held it up to Clam Shell.

"*Xaskwim*," Clam Shell said with a puzzled, incredulous expression as if Tor was asking a foolish question. Clam Shell put his hand to his mouth indicating that it was food.

Tor popped the dried corn kernel into his mouth and bit down. "Ah! That hurts. How can you eat this?" Clam Shell laughed, then pointed to the woman crushing the seeds and put his hand to his mouth. Now Tor understood that you make food from the flour. He just expected the big yellow seeds to be like oats or barley that you could chew.

Clam Shell pointed to the oval ring of long-houses that stood inside the pole wall, including the large open plaza. He pointed out the tall central pole in the plaza and the big fire pit close to it and did a little dance, indicating that this was a place where they held dances.

Next to the pole wall at the easternmost point, away from any other buildings, sat a small conical structure. Tor observed it was built like the long-houses with a bark covering but was barely big enough for a couple of people to get into. The roof was dome-shaped and had a small opening at the top that was stained with soot around the edge, indicating fires were sometimes lit inside it. Clam Shell did not acknowledge it, and Tor wondered if he would know its purpose before they took him to Greenland.

Next, Clam Shell looked at Tor and pointed to the longhouses that had people living in them. He pointed to Wattle's house, then made a sweeping motion to include all the houses. He said, *"Ehes,"* again and swung his hand around the village and back to Wattle's house. Then Clam Shell said, "Tuh?" and pointed to all the houses.

Tor answered, "You want to know where I sleep?" and laid his head on his hands like he was sleeping. Clam Shell smiled and nodded his head vigorously.

"I will tell you where I live!" Tor said loudly, startling Clam Shell. Tor picked up a stick and, in the bare dirt around the fire pit, started drawing pictures of his life over the past moons. Tears began to fill Tor's eyes as he went on. "Many days passed, all of my family, from Ulfrstadt, Norway, loaded into two big ships to move our lives to Greenland! We ran into storms just before we reached Iceland. First, my sister died of a fever, then my mother was killed when the mast broke and a big splinter hit her head, and my father was dragged overboard. I lost my whole family that horrible night. Our broken ship was driven by storm after storm. Finally, the ship broke apart, and I ended up on that beach out there. I have no family, no way to find them. I am lost, lost, lost! What does God want with me?" By now he had dropped to his knees and was sobbing uncontrollably. He put his head in his hands on the ground and cried. Clam Shell tried to console him but did not understand a single word of Tor's Norse.

After a while, Clam Shell finally got Tor to stand up and walked him into Wattle's longhouse, where he could get a drink of water. Clam Shell pointed to where Red Feather sits and to himself said, *"nkahes,"* mother. Then, to where Bear Claw sits and said, *"nux,"* father. Next, to where Strong Wing sits and said, "xansa," older brother. Then, indicated the smaller children and said, *"naxisemes,"* younger brother, younger sister. Next, pointed to where Wattle sits and said *"uma,"* grandmother. She is also *Sakimaxkwe*, Chief". Finally, he pointed to where Long Beard sits and said *"muxumsena,"* grandfather. "We are all the Turkey Clan except grandfather, who is Heron Clan, and Bear Claw, who is of the Bear Clan and born in Mud Town. We all belong to the Turkey People of Willet Village except Bear Claw, who is of the Wolf People. There are three People—Turkey, Turtle, and Wolf People. All the clans in all the villages are these three People. The big villages such as Sun Town and Mud Town have all three People. Some villages have only one People. Round Track, for instance, has only Wolf People clans."

Tor only picked up on the names but understood that they were all family and were important in the village. He pointed to the cooking pots and waved his hand to where the serving girls always positioned themselves and asked, "Thralls?"

Clam Shell cocked his head and said, "*alukakanak*," servants. "They are slaves captured in raids on our enemies' camps."

About that time, Wattle came into the house, followed by Long Beard, Red Feather, Bear Claw, and the servant girls. Old Wattle and Long Beard looked exhausted from the walk across the big field to the campsites of the visitors. As it turned out, the search party was not needed, but the visitors got away later than planned, thanks to the delinquent young adults. It appeared some inter-village marriages might be the result, as often was the case during these big gatherings.

Tor and Clam Shell had gone back outside the palisade, so that Clam Shell could show Tor around some more. They came upon two young men who were working on shaping a canoe. They had a long section of the trunk of a tulip tree split in half with one half lying flat side down on some log blocks. The bark had been peeled off, and they were almost finished with rounding the ends with chopping tools made of flat, sharpened rocks attached to stout sticks. One man finished the rough shaping and, using a large block of sandstone, was scraping the chop marks, smoothing the rounded end of the new boat. Before both ends of the craft had been finished, Clam Shell and Tor had been summoned back to Wattle's house.

"Were you able to find out where he came from and what he wants here?" Wattle asked Clam Shell as he stood before her looking at the floor matting and nervously fidgeting before her. Tor was equally nervous standing behind Clam Shell. Tor stood nearly a head taller than Clam Shell and had a clear view of the old woman and the others questioning the boy. Long Beard, seated to Wattle's left, and Red Feather, on her right, studied Tor intently.

"I think he came from somewhere far, far away, across the Great Ocean in a huge canoe that held a whole village. Storms drove them to our shore. As I understand it, his whole family died as the big canoe broke apart in the sea. Grandmother, I think he is all alone and has lost everything. I could not understand his tongue, but he became extremely upset talking about it. He was shouting, then broke down crying. I feel sorry for him. I brought him in here for some water and corn cakes to settle him down. It must have been a frightening time for him. I admire the way he seems to ignore what must be painful skin. And the bruises he is covered with must give him much pain as he moves around. But he seems to be getting stronger," Clam Shell answered as calmly as he could manage.

Wattle looked at Red Feather, then at Tor, and finally to Long Beard. "What is your opinion of this story, old man?" she asked Long Beard.

"In all the passings of the seasons that I have witnessed, I have never heard a story like this. I know there are old stories and legends about white men and giants and so on. But no one alive has ever seen one of them. I have never seen or even heard of a man that looks anything like this boy. I know that when we found him on the beach, there was some question if he was even alive. There is no doubt he has been through a harrowing experience. I suppose it is possible that there are people who live across the Great Sea in a land where Father Sun starts his journey. It is as if his hair is touched by the sun, and his eyes are like the bluest waters of the sea on a sunny day. Perhaps he is born of Father Sun and some unknown sea goddess," Long Beard said, thinking as he was talking.

"What do you think?" Wattle addressed the question to Red Feather. She would become *Saki-maxkwe* when Wattle passed.

"This is a puzzle we have never been asked to solve. I know of no stories from the old times that deal with strangers from across the Great Sea.

Perhaps Clam Shell misunderstood some of his meaning. In any case, I think his bruising, scratches, and burned skin show that he is of flesh and blood, that he is not some spirit. I think we should keep treating his skin with bear grease and slippery elm bark until he is healed. And feed him until he regains his health. By then, he should learn our tongue enough that he can answer our questions. He has given no indication that he is dangerous, but we should keep an eye on him and not give him any weapons for now," Red Feather stated thoughtfully.

"Your insight and thoughts show you are maturing, daughter," Wattle noted. "We will keep him here as our house guest for now. Make sure his wounds are treated daily, and he is well fed.

"In the meantime, Clam Shell, you will take him out to gather firewood and learn what you can from him and teach him our tongue. Stay close enough to others so that you can get help if you need it. You will give me daily reports on his progress. Our Council will meet soon to discuss his future." She raised her cup of tea toward Tor and said, "Hoo, Tuh!" with a smile.

Tor smiled brightly and said, "Hoo, Uma!" She smiled back.

After a few days, Tor's tormented skin lost most of its soreness, turned dark, and started peeling off in sheets that were striated from all the scratches that had covered him when he arrived. The scabs were shrinking or falling off, leaving fine red lines all over his legs, back, and chest. His bruises were fading to a dark yellow hue. The village people stared at him in wonder.

Eventually, his scratches and bruises healed, and his strength returned. Each day he learned how to speak with the Original People a little more.

CHAPTER 15
TAKEN AWAY

In the middle days of the Moon of Ripening Corn, six canoes from Sun Town arrived at the Willet Village landing. One was a big, wide vessel that belonged to Great Sakimaxkwe Painted Turtle. She sat in the middle on a cushion made from cattail reeds woven tightly together in several layers. Wattle, Long Beard, Red Feather, and Bear Claw stood at the top of the landing to greet her. Strong Wing, Clam Shell, and Tor were in the big field shooting arrows at a target.

"Hoo, Great Sakimaxkwe!" Wattle sounded cheerful, though the knot in her stomach told her this surprise visit could only mean bad news. "We hope that your trip was uneventful and that you enjoy good health on this fine, warm day. The Turkey People and the Turtle People of Willet

Village welcome you to our humble home. Our hunters have been dispersed to bring fresh venison and turkeys for a feast honoring your visit."

"Thank you, Sakimaxkwe Wattle. Your hospitality, as always, is bountiful. I hope this day finds you feeling well and in good spirits," Painted Turtle answered warmly.

They held counsel under an open structure with a thatched roof that provided shade, since it was stiflingly hot in Wattle's longhouse. Soon, venison and turkeys were roasting on spits in the central fire pit in the plaza while they held their counsel in the shaded pavilion. Painted Turtle dismissed everyone except Wattle, Red Feather, and her own daughter, Round Shell, as they talked.

After formal pleasantries were exchanged, Painted Turtle began, "As you are no doubt aware, on the last night of the Solstice Celebration here in Willet Village, many young adults...got to know one another. They were full of excitement from the games and dancing, and many had their first taste of black drink that night. They were feeling heady and without care. Many who would not normally do so ended up coupling in the shadows. This is nothing new—it happens at all our big gatherings. And nothing for us elders to be concerned about. But, as it turns out, that frantic coupling has resulted in my granddaughter,

Willow Branch, being impregnated by your Strong Wing."

She looked straight at Red Feather and said, "I had been planning to marry her to a boy from the Red Wolf Clan, one of the Wolf People clans in Sun Town. I had not yet made formal plans for that wedding, as she had only returned from her first visit to the women's lodge a few days before leaving for the Solstice Celebration. My daughter, Round Shell here, said that Willow Branch was not ready for marriage yet. Perhaps I should not have taken her counsel." Painted Turtle looked everyone in the eyes as she continued.

"In talking with Willow Branch, and to Round Shell, it seems that Willow Branch thinks she is very much in love with your Strong Wing. She claims that he is the only young man she has shared a blanket with. And though he is also quite young, a marriage between them makes sense. The question is when. The sooner the better, I have determined. Willow Branch will soon be filling out a dress, and a young girl would rather not look like a sow bear on her wedding day. Normally, I would wait for *Gamwing*, but that celebration is already too full." She smiled coyly as she spoke.

Red Feather looked stunned. She had not given one heartbeat's thought to Strong Wing getting married to anyone, let alone the Great Sakimaxkwe's granddaughter. That would mean his moving to Sun Town.

"Great Sakimaxkwe, I understand your thoughts on this matter completely and am in favor of strengthening the bond between Sun Town and Willet Village. My only concern is, with the recent Solstice Celebration and your annual tribute to be paid right after harvest, I am not sure Willet Village can afford a bride price right now. I will need to take this up with our Council. So, if you tell me your demands, I will see how soon we can meet them," Wattle said carefully.

Painted Turtle smiled. She looked over to see Strong Wing, Clam Shell, and Tor walking into the village, each carrying a bow and quiver. She guessed they were going to Wattle's lodge for tea. "I think the solution is quite simple. What I want for your bride price is the yellow-haired boy."

"What could you possibly want with him?" Wattle replied, a puzzled look on her face. "He only eats, drinks, and sleeps. His tongue is completely foreign to ours. When he is talking and has a word or phrase that he cannot say, he just uses one from his old tongue. Most of the time I cannot under-stand anything that comes out of his mouth. He is a slow learner to our ways, and we do not trust him with weapons. I am still not sure what to do with him. He is probably best used as a household slave," she said flippantly, trying to downplay his achievements and worth. Red Feather furtively looked at her mother with disbelief in her eyes. Painted Turtle picked up on the glance immediately.

"Nevertheless, he is the price I am demanding. We are prepared to take him with us tomorrow. The wedding will take place ten days from today. Please have Strong Wing in Sun Town in nine days. We will have a two-day feast to celebrate the union. You are welcome to bring as many from Willet Village as you like. Also, the Willet Village tribute will be cut in half this harvest and from now on to honor the new bond between Sun Town and Willet Village." Painted Turtle was matter of fact and final on the issue, leaving no room for negotiations.

Wattle was not sure if she had won or lost. Certainly, she was losing a warrior, but Strong Wing was young and still unproven. Losing Tor would mean one less mouth to feed, although she was becoming endeared with him. He was working hard to please her and was quickly learning the ways of the Lenape. She could see his potential as a great warrior.

Tor started to ask Strong Wing how the elders could make such life-changing decisions for young people without even asking their opinion. Then he thought of the customs in his homeland. Father was off in Greenland when Grandfather decided to marry him to someone Father had never met. And all the thralls the Norse families owned were taken without choice from their families and homelands. Tor, himself, was now basically just a thrall. He understood that much. Now he would be taken to a new place and be under the control of someone new. It hardly seemed fair. He was just learning how to get along with the people in Willet Village. It was apparent to him that no one in these lands cared if he ever returned home.

———

"TAKE THESE THINGS. We had planned to adopt you into the Turkey Clan at the Equinox, and these were to be your new clan buckskins. Now you will become Turtle Clan in Sun Town. Painted Turtle will object to these, but I do not care. You were found and rescued by Turkey Clan, and these are a gift from us to you," Wattle said, a note of exasperation in her voice.

"I will wear them with honor, Grandmother," Tor replied stoically. He feared what awaited him in Sun Town.

"The Solstice Celebration will be in Sun Town next summer. It will be a pleasure watching you in the pahsaheman," Wattle answered him with glassy eyes. "Now we had better go to the landing before Painted Turtle storms in here to get you." Wattle handed him a woven cattail bag with the new clothes and a few other things. "There are some of your favorite corn cakes flavored with honey in the bag." He picked up his child's war club, bow, and quiver. After a last look around, Tor followed everyone out of the lodge.

Bright-Eyed Boy broke the somber silence. "I cannot see why Strong Wing and Tuh both must leave. One should stay here to teach me!"

Red Feather took his hand and quietly said, "One day you will understand, son." She was holding back her own tears.

Clam Shell broke in, "That task will fall to me, little brother! You are in good hands."

CHAPTER 16

BRIDE PRICE

I t took two days of paddling and portaging to reach the Lenape River. They would arrive at Sun Town on the fourth day after that, leaving three days to prepare for the wedding. Tor made it a point to wear his new buckskin shirt and leggings, even though he was too hot with them on.

Painted Turtle took the time to quiz Tor on what he had learned about the Original People. She explained to him that in Willet Village, there were the Turkey and the Turtle Peoples, with several clans within each group. But in Sun Town, there were also the Wolf People. Each village had its own makeup of the three peoples. Round Track, for instance, only had six clans of Wolf People. Slider Village was made up of only Turtle People. It had taken Painted Turtle two days to teach Tor the organization of the villages and towns on the rivers, and the different organizations among the Original People both to the north and south of her domain.

The first day on the river, Painted Turtle continued her conversations with Tor. She had been somewhat impressed and found herself quite attached to him by the time they were on the Lenape River. She began, "I see you have crafted yourself a child's bow, arrows, and a quiver. You even have a small war club. Do you feel like you are becoming a man?"

"I helped Bear Claw make the bow and some of the arrow points. I am not skilled enough with the straightener to make good arrows yet. And Red Feather made the quiver. I have so much to learn," Tor answered, betraying melancholy in his voice.

"Do you like your weapons? Can you use them?" she inquired.

"They are all right, but not as good as in my homeland. I had a good sword and a bow with steel-tipped arrows that were of much better quality. A Norse battle axe would cut through the skin and wood shields your warriors carry as if cutting through grass," he replied nonchalantly.

She paused. "Should I worry about your

warriors coming here to destroy me for taking you into my household?"

"Ha! Practically everyone I ever knew is dead. No one is left who knows, or cares, what happened to me. I see no hope of ever returning to my home, nor do I even have a home to return to." He looked away and down with a sob.

Noting his distress, Painted Turtle asked, "These weapons you talk of. What makes them so much better than ours?"

He sniffed back his sorrow, wiped his eyes on his shirt, and spoke, "It is the steel. Our weapons are made of hard metal. Like copper, except it is much harder. It will hold a sharp edge, even in battle where weapons clang against each other hard and often. Our steel arrow points are heavier and sink deeper into anything they hit. And our shields are thick, able to stop those arrows and blows from battle-axes. Our warriors form a V-shaped wall with those shields that can stop a charging army." He used his hands to demonstrate some of his points.

"It sounds as if you are homesick," she replied in a motherly tone. "I am sorry, but none of us know anything about your homeland or how to take you there. As you have seen, our canoes are not made to travel across the Great Ocean. You will need to decide whether to live in sadness for what was or to make the most of your new home. Our traditions are full of stories of great men and women who were thrust into new lives and became the heroes we strive to emulate. Tomorrow maybe you can tell me more about this metal you speak of."

Without hesitation, Tor began an explanation of the iron-making process. "We harvest great quantities of peat from local bogs. That peat is rich in iron. I see similar bogs just back from the river in low areas along this river. The peat is roasted over a bed of hot coals that burns up most of the plant material. Then, what is left is gathered and mixed with charcoal and put in special kilns. A bladder made of animal hide is attached to the bottom of those kilns to blow air into the coals, creating extreme heat. They are heated, burning the charcoal and charred matter at that high temperature. The globs of iron drip down to the bottom of the kilns and form a blossom.

"When the blossom is cooled, a section of the kiln is removed, and the blossom is taken to the smithy where it is heated until it glows orange. The worker—a big, strong man—beats it with a big iron hammer, continually reheating it, folding it and turning it. He does this until the impurities are forced out of the steel. Once the steel is formed, the blacksmith can make products, such as tools, fittings, spears, and arrow points. The highest quality steel is further worked and pounded, layer after layer, to make swords and axes for war. The bogs around our home seem to form an extremely hard and resilient steel that people from all over come to trade for."

"You seem to know much about the process. Do you think you could make that metal here?" she asked.

"I do not see how. It takes fire much, much hotter than any I have seen here. More importantly, it takes a man who knows how to heat the iron and just how to fold and bend it. I have watched but have none of those skills. A blacksmith serves as an apprentice for several sun cycles before he is ready to make the simplest of tools. Producing weapons takes a master. Do you understand?" Tor replied.

During the explanation, it dawned on Tor how much he had aged in the less than six months since he left Norway. It seemed like years since they had set sail from Ulfrstadt.

"Yes, I think I understand. Many of the words you use are foreign to me, despite your fine use of sign language, but I get the point that it takes people trained and familiar with making the hard metal, and we do not have those kinds of people. Our skill ends with heating certain rocks in red coals long enough to melt pure copper out of them. This hard metal is beyond my understanding," Painted Turtle answered.

Over the remaining days of their trip to Sun Town, Painted Turtle continued to question Tor about the world he left behind and teach him about the world he found himself in.

CHAPTER 17
SUN TOWN

As they approached Sun Town, four days later, several canoes joined to escort them to the landing. Tor was awed by the size of the town. It was bigger than Ulfrstadt. Smoke from all the campfires hung like a cloud over the valley. The pole wall enveloped twice as much land as Willet Village, and there were many more houses amid the trees and open places outside the village. Other than one large field, every open space was filled with ripening corn, beans, and squash.

Painted Turtle explained that he would be welcomed into the village and soon the Turtle Clan Council would meet to decide whether to adopt him into the clan. She told him that from what she had seen, there would be no problems, and the adoption would take place at the Gamwing, *or Big House Celebration*. She told him that the celebration was held in each village and town once a sun cycle. Not all towns held their Gamwing at the same time. For instance, in Sun Town, it was held along with the harvest, or *Green Corn* celebration, in the early fall, only a moon away. In Willet and some other villages, Gamwing was held in midwinter. Others held it in spring just before the Planting Moon and had fertility ceremonies. In the meantime, there would be much to do over the next few days in preparation of the wedding between Willow Branch and Strong Wing.

"I know of some couples who married in Willet Village, and there was no ceremony or feast. The woman just accepted the man and some gifts into her mother's house, then the couple went to the 'wedding house' and went on a deer hunt. That was pretty much it. Why is Strong Wing and Willow Branch's wedding different?" Tor asked.

"To start with, it is 'Willow Branch and Strong Wing.' We always say the woman first," Painted Turtle stated.

"I do not know if I will ever get used to that. Where I come from, it all belongs to the man. Everything revolves around the man. He owns the property and makes all the decisions. Here it is so different. Do not get me wrong, there are some strong women in our society, even warriors, or 'shieldmaidens.' My father respected my mother and gave in to her will often. But as a rule, it is a man's world," Tor replied.

"I like that term, shieldmaiden," Painted Turtle quipped. She then continued her previous explanation, "There are some peoples who put the man first in these lands, too. Some of the warlike *Minquas* to our north put the man first. I do not know how they do it. That is probably why they are always on the trail of war.

"To answer your question, the marriage between Willow Branch and Strong Wing signals the bonding of two peoples, the Turtle and the Turkey People, two clans, the Turtle and Turkey Clans, and two villages, Sun Town and Willet Village. Such a bond is unusual and cause for special celebration. Otherwise, their marriage will be like all others.

"She will make a special corn stew in one bowl. He will come to our lodge dressed in new clothes to impress her. Of course, she will be in her new wedding dress. She will accept him by inviting him in to share the stew with her, which they will share from the same bowl, using only fingers. After the stew, they will lie together in the special wedding lodge. Afterward, they will meet well-wishers and receive gifts, then go out into the forest to the southwest where he will hunt deer to demonstrate he is a good provider. Normally, they would stay out for up to two moons, but since she is already with child, they will return as soon as they eat the first animal he kills. They will move into my longhouse for a time. If they decide to build their own lodge, it will be his responsibility. He will probably rely on you to help him with that."

"I will be happy to help my brother in any way I can," Tor answered solemnly.

"With such an important marriage, we will celebrate and feast for two days, bestowing many songs and gifts on the Creator and the other gods so that they will want to bless and bring good fortune to this union," Painted Turtle looked to the sky as she talked.

"And why do you get me as a gift for the marriage?" Tor asked innocently.

"Surely you understand that I am the Great Sakimaxkwe, the chief of all the river towns and villages of the people, the Turtle Clan, the Turtle People, the Wolf People, and Sun Town?" she asked.

"Yes, I understand that Sun Town is the biggest village among the Original People on the rivers and that you are the great chief, but it seems that Round Shell would receive gifts for Willow

Branch's marriage since she is her mother," Tor stated in a quizzical manner.

"Round Shell is my daughter, so everything she has belongs to me until I die. Since she is in my household, all that is hers is mine. For that reason, the wedding gifts are presented to me, and I decide how to distribute them. Some will go to the bride, some to her mother. I choose which ones, if any, I wish to keep, and the rest will be distributed back to the clans. You were the gift I wanted. I am fascinated by your story. I want to help and watch you become one of the Original People. I think you will be a great warrior.

"The gifts are presented through the clans, not individual families. But you are welcome, as Strong Wing's adopted brother, to give him some gift, if you choose. It could be a turtle-shell rattle, a knife, or special arrow, something of that nature," Painted Turtle explained.

"My fa...er...mother and father, each told me their own versions of their wedding. It was like Willow Branch's. They both belonged to important families from different towns. Father was the son of the jarl—a kind of chief—of Ulfrland, and she was the niece of the jarl of Bierkland. Their celebration lasted seven days, but the bride and groom were compelled to stay intoxicated for a moon.

Nine moons later, I was born," Tor waxed melancholic in a distant voice.

Tor thought about many things as they slid onto the sandy canoe landing. His fear of the dugouts was long gone, and he athletically hopped out as they slid to a stop. Then he assisted Painted Turtle with her egress. Many had gathered to welcome them home and to get a look at Tor.

At Painted Turtle's left side, Tor passed through the overlapped pole wall. As Sun Town was surrounded by a double pole wall, about four paces apart, it was necessary to pass through a second such opening to finally make it into the village. He found out that a stronger defense was deemed necessary because the Minquas were becoming more brazen with their raids, though none had attacked Sun Town yet.

Once inside, he noted the differences between Sun Town and Willet Village. There were more big lodges. Each was marked with a sentry post displaying a carved clan figure near the top. Painted Turtle's Turtle Clan lodge was the biggest. The clan lodges were in three clusters, the Turtle People being the largest cluster. In the center of the plaza was a Big House. It was bigger than Painted Turtle's lodge and almost square. It had doors on the east and west sides, three sentry posts near the east entrance, and two posts off to the side about three paces apart. A lintel positioned overhead connected those posts. A little farther east and to the side was a single pole on the edge of a fire pit. There were marks on it where ropes had been tied many times at a height higher than a man is tall. Dark stains streaked down from the rope marks. Tor guessed that this pole was where a bear or deer would be hung and butchered as part of the Gamwing next moon.

Smaller longhouses rimmed the inside of the pole wall with the usual latrines, trash pits, individual burial plots, and screening bushes between the lodges and the wall. A square building sat behind the Turtle, Turkey, and Wolf Clan lodges. Tor had learned from Willet Village that these were the charnel houses where important clan members' bodies were prepared for the afterlife and their bones laid on special racks awaiting burial in certain ceremonies. Sweat lodges were located next to each of the clan and men's society longhouses.

Like Willet Village, the usual activities were being carried out around Sun Town—children playing, women sitting at looms weaving, women pounding corn in wooden mortars with log pestles, and men sitting around making arrows or tools while they smoked clay pipes. The buildings were constructed the same way, with pole frames, high domed roofs with smoke holes along the center, and bark slab walls held down with a grid of smaller saplings.

When they went into Painted Turtle's long-house, Tor was introduced to Round Shell, Round Shell's older daughter, Willow Branch, her younger daughter, Small Dove, and her son of only four summers, Plum. Also present was Painted Turtle's father, Long Lance. Long Lance had seen six-tens-and-five summers and was white-haired, toothless, and feeble. He was nearly blind and could no longer hear. He only communicated in sign language, and only with Painted Turtle and Round Shell.

Willow Branch was sewing colored beads and quills in chevrons on an almost white, richly tanned doeskin shirt. Round Shell was making a wampum belt for Willow Branch's wedding skirt.

Tor learned that Painted Turtle's husband, Black Spike, had died two winters earlier from a wound he had gotten from a mountain lion that had been invaded with angry demons. In addition to her only daughter, Round Shell, Painted Turtle had three sons who lived with their wives in their own lodges. Round Shell's husband, Blue Goose, and ten others were out hunting deer for the wedding feast.

CHAPTER 18
STRONG WING'S WEDDING

Two days later, twenty canoes arrived from Willet Village. Strong Wing and Green Shell paddled Wattle's wide canoe heaped with baskets of clothes and food, along with Wattle and Long Beard. Bear Claw and Clam Shell paddled a canoe carrying Red Feather, Little Star, and Bright-Eyed Boy. Everything they needed for the next few days was in bags, baskets, and jars, all jammed into the big dugouts. They went to a point about halfway along the large clearing where they would set up tents above the river, by the narrow band of trees lining the river-bank. The town's young people had gathered an adequate supply of firewood and kindling for their campfires.

Tor rushed to greet his friends from Willet

Village. Each was happy to see him, even the little children who had been so afraid of him when he first arrived in Willet Village. Now they clung to him like a close relative. Only Strong Wing seemed nervous and apprehensive about being in Sun Town.

Tor helped put up their tents, which consisted of tanned and hairless deer hides sewn together hung over poles placed in a circle then tied near the top, forming a conical shape. The tents only provided covered space for sleeping and storage of essential items. Almost everything else was packed in baskets and bags and covered with skins. A few items were hung from tree limbs to keep raccoons and skunks from getting to them. Guards would be posted at night and when they were in the village to keep snakes, crows, jays, raccoons, skunks, opossums, bears, wolves, and coyotes away.

The day of the wedding came soon enough. It was a clear morning with a light south breeze. By midday, it would be hot and humid. Everyone was bustling around, making sure everything would be ready for the feast. Blue Goose and his party had returned with eight fat deer. Two had late fawns, still suckling, which were also harvested. Among other things, their small hooves would make good rattles for men to tie onto their legs for the dances to come in the fall and winter, and the soft skins would make linings for winter breechclouts and baby clothes.

Bear Claw, Clam Shell, and Tor helped Strong Wing prepare himself. They spent two hands of time in the sweat lodge basking in cedar berry and mint-scented steam. Next, Strong Wing's body was slathered with a mixture of bear grease, mint, and cedar oil. His head was shaved except for a long roach on the back of his head. He had earned this honor by killing a large bear. The bear's claws and canine teeth were displayed on a necklace he wore. His roach was combed with a small amount of mint-scented bear grease until it shone and then braided and allowed to hang down his back. A single turkey feather was entwined with a copper coil and allowed to hang from the base of his roach. The copper coil also supported a deer-tail comb that stretched from the roach over his head to the top of his forehead. The deer hair had been shaved to make a narrow, tall, dense comb. The bases of the white hairs were dyed black and the tips red.

One side of his head was painted with a red, strutting turkey and the other side, a white one. He had a single turkey track tattooed on each temple such that one day he would sport a row of them walking from his temples to the center of his forehead. Another tattoo consisted of a series of dots from each ear and over the bridge of his nose. A tattoo in the image of an attacking goshawk sat at the top of his sternum, another of a strutting turkey just below that. A new, finely tanned, and quilled buckskin breechclout hung on his waist. Over that was placed a flap of black-and-white-checked wampum, the top of which was made as a belt. Beaded armlets made up of geometric patterns of the four sacred colors—black, white, green, and yellow—were placed halfway up each upper arm. His feet were clad in finely tanned buckskin moccasins with fringed edges and fawn-hoof rattles on the top of each foot.

Tor reached into his shoulder bag and pulled out an item wrapped in rabbit skin and presented it to Strong Wing. Strong Wing rolled it open to reveal an obsidian knife with a blade as long as Strong Wing's hand. It was hafted onto a deer antler handle that displayed rawhide strips in the four sacred colors wrapped around the butt end. The sheath was also beaded in stripes of black, white, green, and yellow.

"It's beautiful! Where did you get it? I know you did not have time to make it yourself since you have been here," Strong Wing asked Tor.

"I made a deal to provide firewood all winter to the elder who did make it," Tor replied. "It was all I could think of that would be worthy."

"Thank you." Strong Wing said, unable to take his eyes off the knife.

Bear Claw went to a long bag and took out a new elm and sinew bow and buckskin quiver containing twelve chokecherry arrows with triangular flint hunting points attached. "This is to help you keep your new woman well fed. I do not want my grandson starving because that old bow of yours is too weak to kill a deer. With this bow, I know you will be able to provide well for your family."

"You two make a man want to get married every day!" Strong Wing chuckled.

"This is for one time only," Bear Claw replied. They would have hugged, but it would have messed up Strong Wing's wedding attire.

"I only have this," Clam Shell said meekly as he handed Strong Wing a small bundle of tanned rabbit skin. Wrapped inside the skin was a goshawk's foot with the talons spread like it was attacking prey.

"My spirit helper! Thank you, little brother. I will keep it in my spirit bundle always," Strong Wing said solemnly.

Strong Wing looked at Tor. "I need a drink,"

"Just happen to have some fresh sassafras tea flavored with mint and blackberries," Tor answered, turning to a jar he had brought from

Painted Turtle's hearth earlier. The four of them had just finished their tea when they heard little feet padding toward them. Little Star poked her head into the groom's four-sided dressing place, a shelter that Bear Claw and Tor had made from vertical poles covered with cattail mats.

"Are you ever going to be ready?" Little Star asked impatiently. "We want to see what you look like before you get taken away by that girl!" When she saw Strong Wing, she exclaimed, "Strong Wing? Is that you? I never saw you look like that! Where did you get all those beads? And your hair looks funny! He-he!" She giggled.

"You'll have to leave if you are going to make fun of me, little one. Where's my war club?" he growled at her.

"Ayeeeee!" she screamed and ran out.

The men moved to the campfire circle so Red Feather and Wattle could look Strong Wing over. "You look almost as good as I once did," Long Beard spoke up first. "You remember that day, old woman?" The old man turned to Wattle.

"No one cares what you used to look like, old man. This is the boy's day, and he looks fit to be War Chief of the Turkey People!" Wattle said proudly.

Red Feather just looked on with a tear in her

eye. She could not believe this day had come so quickly. "Amazing," she finally whispered.

Just then, a conch-shell horn sounded from inside the pole wall signifying it was time for the groom to make his entrance. He would come into the village, walk to each clan elder, and introduce himself.

Wattle, Red Feather, Long Beard, Bear Claw, Clam Shell, Bright-Eyed Boy, Little Star, and Tor followed a few paces behind Strong Wing. Tor watched everything Strong Wing did. After greeting the elders, Strong Wing walked proudly into the longhouse where Willow Branch waited to accept him and offer her special corn stew. The two would sit beside each other and eat the stew from the same bowl using their fingers. Next, they would go to the wedding lodge set apart at the edge of the plaza away from the longhouses. They would lie together in the wigwam and come out together when they were satisfied with each other.

After the wedding lodge, they would take up their packs and start their deer hunt. They would stay out, camping and hunting, until she was comfortable with his ability to provide meat for her and her family.

Willow Branch's hair was wound into a multilay-ered bun on top of her head and held in place with turkey bone and copper pins, signifying she was a woman and no longer a maiden. Strands of cloth dyed in the sacred colors flowed down her back. She wore a sleeveless doeskin shirt decorated with turtles painted in the four sacred colors around the neck and along the lower, fringed hem. Over the shoulders and down the front were chevrons of porcupine quills and colored shell beads. Some of the quills were in a black and white pattern, others in the four sacred colors. The shirt hung down over a doeskin skirt that was decorated similarly except for the bottom hem, which was trimmed with a band of black and white-checked wampum just above the fringes. The shirt was tied around the waist with a wide wampum belt of the same black and white-checked pattern. Several shell necklaces of varying length hung from her neck. On her feet, she wore light-colored tanned buckskin moccasins with a fringed hem around the foot and beaded strings on top.

Once the couple disappeared into the woods, everyone moved back into the open plaza next to the Big House and the feast started, to be followed by dancing well into the night.

CHAPTER 19
BECOMING A MAN

With the marriage of Strong Wing and Willow Branch out of the way, Painted Turtle could concentrate on the Gamwing and all its activities. It was important to her to get Tor adopted into the Turtle Clan and, officially, into her household. She had less than a moon to make everything perfect.

One matter that disturbed her was Tor's name. She had tried, unsuccessfully, to learn the proper pronunciation of the simple word. Try as she might, she simply could not train her tongue to make the "r" sound the way he did—it always came out "Tuh" or "Tuheh." She knew that was not correct and wanted him to feel completely at home.

She met with the shaman of Sun Town to

discuss her concerns. She was surprised to learn that Wild Crow was also quite interested in Tor's story and had spoken with the youth several times. Wild Crow had given Tor the knife he presented to Strong Wing on his wedding day.

"His story of survival out there on the Great Ocean is truly the work of spirits. Surely he has been brought to our lands for reasons we can only guess. I, too, have great difficulty trying to say his name as he says it. I have given this much thought," Wild Crow explained.

"Do you think it would be proper to have a naming ceremony at the Big House Celebration, when we officially adopt him into the Turkey Clan?" Painted Turtle asked.

"You are seeing my thoughts, Great Saki-maxkwe. Normally, we would send a boy his age out into the forest to fast and fend for himself for days, and depending on what he has to say upon return, it would be my place to name him based on that experience. But the young man we are discussing was lost on that sea where he experienced several fasts, had spirit dreams, was saved by dolphins, and survived it all. Since arriving in our lands, he has learned our tongue quickly, though not perfectly yet. He has adapted to our ways better than I would have if the roles were reversed. His skill with our weapons far exceeds that of many of our own youth who have grown up with them. I am ready to name him as a man and bring him into our people. He has seen ten and three summers. Too young to enter our warrior society, but he will be ready sooner than we think. I will name him if you so wish, at the Big House ceremony, Great Sakimaxkwe.

"Wild Crow, I do wish that, and thank you for easing my mind on the subject. Shall I tell him that he will be given a man's name at the adoption ceremony?" she asked tentatively.

"I cannot see a reason why not unless you want to surprise him. Would that be wise?" the shaman inquired.

"I will make sure he does not come to you wanting to know his new name before the ceremony. He is baffled by some of our customs. He says that in his homeland—he calls it 'The Father Land'—they name their children as soon as they know they will live. He was named after some old great god because his father liked that name. And he thinks our ways are odd," she mused.

"All peoples have different ways, my lady. It would be odd if we were all the same and much less interesting," he replied.

"You are right, of course. Thank you for discussing this with me."

"One more thing, Great Sakimaxkwe. If I were

you, I would avoid making any plans for him to marry any of our young maidens," he said seriously.

"Oh? Why do you say that shaman?" she asked with a hint of surprise. "I surely have not given that much thought but wonder why you would caution me at this point."

"Just that, in my discussions with him, he desperately wants to find a way to this Greenland, where he says they were going when their great canoe was blown off course by storms. And there is the part when I said Power must have something in mind for him—some greater purpose for coming here. I cannot see random storms bringing a body across the Great Ocean like that. It has never happened in the past. Why now? I would wager the Thunderers were acting on behalf of some greater spirit. To tie him to clan responsibilities may not be what they have in mind," Wild Crow explained.

"I see. Something to think about. But he is so young. Surely there will be time before the gods come calling for him," she declared.

"I would not try to outguess what the gods are thinking, my lady," he cautioned.

"Of course, you are right, Wild Crow. I thank you again and will talk to you again before the Gamwing." She turned and left his lodge.

Later that night, when the family finished their evening meal of rabbit stew and corn cakes flavored with acorn butter and blueberries, Painted Turtle looked at Tor and said, "Would you like to go for a walk? I have some things to talk to you about in private."

Tor noted that everyone looked at her with inquiring eyes, then turned to him. He shrugged his shoulders and answered, "Of course, Great Sakimaxkwe." He especially caught the look of jealousy in Round Shell's eyes.

Once out of the longhouse and away from quizzical ears, she asked, "So, how are you getting along? Are you feeling welcome here? I can tell you are making good progress learning our tongue."

"Fine. I am glad Strong Wing is here now. That gives me a friend to do things with. We are both strangers here, so we have that. I can draw his bow now and think it is time for me to build a man's bow for myself. Mine is fine for rabbits and squirrels, but I would not want to run into a bear with it," Tor answered evenly. He was curious as to why she wanted to talk to him alone.

"As you know, the Big House Celebration is less than a half moon away. On the second day, we are going to have an adoption rite that will make you a permanent member of the Turtle Clan and my household. You will have a home for as long as you desire to stay here. And if you leave, you will be welcome any time you come back." Painted Turtle carefully spoke her words so that he would understand their meaning.

"Where would I go? I have nowhere to go in this land, and no one waits for me anywhere. My great-uncle in Greenland is convinced by now that no one survived our voyage across the sea. No one else would even know who I am," he answered, sadness in his voice.

"I, we, want you to be happy here. I talked to Wild Crow today. He says you have talked to him many times since you came among us. He likes you very much. He says that the storms that pushed you across the Great Ocean were out of the ordinary, that the spirits brought you here for a purpose we can only guess. Do you have any idea about that?" she quizzed Tor.

"All I know is how frightening things became. Iceland was right there before us. The sky turned black, waterspouts were everywhere, and then a great wall of water descended on us, driving us farther and farther from our destination. It was horrible!" Tor was getting emotional with the memory.

Painted Turtle hugged him to her. "You are safe here, Tuh. We won't let anything like that happen here," she assured him in her motherly voice.

"No, no one is safe anywhere. Bad things can happen, no matter who or how strong you are. No one was stronger or more prepared than my father, and by chance a splinter from the big tree in our great canoe caught him and took him overboard to his death. No one could be ready for that, nor could they stop it," Tor reflected hopelessly. "When it is time, I will know when and where I am needed."

"To change the subject, you are very aware that we have difficulty pronouncing your name properly. In fact, none of us can. You know that our customs dictate that when a boy is about your age, he takes his man's name that follows him the rest of his life. The child is no more, and it is the same with the child's name. We thought we would include a naming ceremony with the adoption rites at the Big House Celebration. What do you think of that?" she asked with an upbeat tone.

"Fine. In the fatherland, we are given a name when we prove we will live. That usually takes place any time from one to three moons. If a child is sickly for a long time but lives, sometimes a name is not given for a whole sun cycle or more. That name is given to our god and lasts our whole lifetime. But I am no longer among my people, so whatever your customs are will be alright for me," Tor replied.

"But did you not tell me that sometimes a man gets a new name as an adult? Like someone named 'Eik Toglooskun' who changed to 'Eik the Ued?'" she asked.

"You mean 'Erik Thorgglesson' became 'Erik The Red.' Yes, and his son, 'Leif Eriksson' is called 'Leif The Lucky.' Those are only nicknames. Sort of like how Strong Wing has started calling Willow Branch 'Big Belly.' It is not her real name. If I did ever get back among my own people, I would be known as 'Tor Eriksson,' no matter what name I am known by here. Do you understand?"

"I think so. You will be given a new man's name in the Big House, regardless—we need a name for you that we can pronounce. According to our ways, Wild Crow will give you a name that fits your unique situation, and it will last while you are with us. Do you think that is fair?"

"It is. I will do as your customs dictate. That is how it will be, always," he replied.

They turned and went back to her longhouse in silence.

CHAPTER 20
A NEW NAME

The Big House Celebration started four days before the fall equinox. All the corn, beans, and squash—the "three sisters" —had been harvested. The big ceremonial house in the center of the Sun Town plaza was packed to overflowing, and the entire building was surrounded by people four rows deep who were eager to hear what was taking place inside.

The first afternoon was taken up by clan business, as each clan reported on the harvest of the three sisters and if any shortages of winter food supplies were expected. After the reports were completed, a feast of roasted green corn, the first corn of the season, was served around the central fire pit in the plaza.

As darkness fell, drums began pounding from within the building. Costumed dancers filed in from the back and began dancing in lines around the center. Men in gaudy skins and feathers formed a circle in the center and danced, stomping feet, shaking torsos and decorated arms to the beat of the drums. Each man wore a distinctive mask that depicted either terror or happiness, depending on how one looked at it. After the men circled four times in one direction, a line of similarly clad women came in circling the men in the opposite direction four times. More dancers arrived snaking in and out of the gyrating bodies.

At some signal, unknown to Tor, the drums stopped, and the dancers dropped to one knee in one motion. From his place on the raised platform, Tor noted the walls were lined with children of all ages. When all got quiet, a huffing noise was heard from the back. Suddenly, a big bear appeared and went down the line of children, scaring them with growls and the clacking of a turtle-shell rattle. The adults roared with laughter while the children screamed in fear. Satisfied the children were sufficiently frightened, the bear quickly ran out the east door.

The dancing continued with groups of dancers replacing the ones who had already participated. Tor did not recognize anyone dancing, although he knew Strong Wing and Willow Branch were in there somewhere. Her costume adequately covered her growing belly. Those strange and sometimes hideous masks were a good disguise.

The dancing continued well into the night. When the final drumbeat sounded, everyone was exhausted. The building had become sweltering, and the odor of sweaty bodies overwhelmed Tor's senses. The final groups of dancers were covered with paint that had run with their sweat, leaving their costumes so soaked, they were barely recognizable. As they filed out, they pulled off their masks so they could finally breathe clean air. The first gray light of a new day was visible over the eastern palisade wall.

Tor was glad to get to his newly constructed sleeping platform along the south wall of the Turtle Clan longhouse. He was asleep before his head hit the sleeping skins.

The next day, the whole process began again when the sun was at its highest point in the early autumn sky. So far, the celebration had been blessed with warm days, cool nights, and clear skies.

After a ceremonial pipe smoking and prayer by Wild Crow, Tor and Painted Turtle were ushered to the center of the building.

Tor was dressed in a new buckskin, long-sleeved ceremonial shirt with long fringes along the sleeves, across the shoulders, and around the bottom hem. The shirt was decorated with beads and quill chevrons down the chest and sleeves. The back featured a large, dyed image of a red and black turtle. The shirt came down to his upper thighs and was tied at the waist with a hemp belt covered with blue and white wampum. His new sheathed knife and war club hung on the belt. He wore matching buckskin leggings with fringe down the outer legs and each thigh decorated with beads of the four sacred colors in the shape of turtles. New high moccasins sporting quillwork chevrons and fawn-hoof rattles on the top of the foot adorned his feet.

Painted Turtle wore a yellow-dyed doeskin dress that hung to her lower calves. It featured elaborate beadwork, shellwork, and quillwork from the shoulders to below the knees. A hemp belt covered with indigo bunting feathers was tied around her slender waist. Many ropes of shell beads hung in various lengths from her neck, and a copper band with a carved turtle image was centered on her throat. Her hair was wound into a tight bun on the back of her head and pinned with copper skewers. A small medicine bundle with a turtle image painted on leather was fitted to the crown of her head. Woven leather thong armbands dyed in the four sacred colors decorated her upper arms. Many bracelets of small, colored beads and copper covered both wrists. Her moccasins matched her dress and had beads of the four sacred colors embroidered in the shape of turtles on the top of each foot. She had narrow white and red stripes painted on her forehead and cheeks indicating she was a new mother, albeit past the age of childbearing.

Wild Crow took up the ceremonial pipe and drew in air in while a boy held a burning ember to the bowl filled with fresh sacred tobacco. Blue smoke was puffed to the four directions, the underworld, and the sky while a prayer was chanted to the Creator. Next, the shaman gave a long dissertation on how Painted Turtle had brought Tor to Sun Town and all the things the boy had achieved since his arrival. The blue smoke was, again, puffed to the four directions, the underworld, and the sky while a prayer was chanted to various gods.

Next, Wild Crow handed the pipe to Painted Turtle, who repeated those actions except for the talk about Tor. Then she chanted a blessing to Mother Earth, giver of children to families of all the clans.

She then summoned the Turtle Clan elders to come to the center and stand behind her. When all had assembled, she spoke to everyone in the building. "People of Sun Town, the Council of Elders of the Turtle Clan, of the Turtle People, of Sun Town, and the nation of the Original People do, at this time, declare that we have taken this foreign boy into our hearts and now make him a member of our family and clan from this day forward."

The crowd roared a loud, "Hoo!" in recognition of the adoption.

Wild Crow looked at Tor, then turned to the gathered crowd. "The person you see before you has performed all the things our ancestors deemed necessary to become a man among the Turtle Clan, of the Turtle People, of Sun Town, and the Original People." The shaman laid an eagle wing on Tor's head, shook it ceremoniously and declared, "The boy known to us as 'Tuh' is no more. The boy is replaced by the man, and his name is 'Yellow Hair.' From this moment on, we will all know and address him by this name." The entire crowd lifted their voices to shout, "*Hoo!* Yellow Hair!" The sound reverberated past the palisade into the surrounding forest.

Tor glanced around. Upon seeing all eyes on him, felt his face burn as he blushed at the recognition of his new name. He gathered himself, spread his arms, palms up, and stoically called out, "Hoo!" loud enough for all to hear.

The Gamwing festivities continued for another eight days.

CHAPTER 21
FIGHTING MINQUAS

The next several weeks were busy as the clans prepared Sun Town for winter. Tor, now Yellow Hair, spent most days with Strong Wing hunting, setting snares, or gathering firewood. He fulfilled his promise to Wild Crow, making sure the shaman had plenty of firewood for the cold days ahead.

One day, Yellow Hair and Strong Wing were hunting northwest of Sun Town. The night had been cold, and the day was cloudy with a blustery north wind. They picked up an elk track and were following it. Strong Wing came up with a plan where he could go off the trail, cut off the elk, and send it in Yellow Hair's direction. Yellow Hair took his post while Strong Wing made a circuitous route to a stand of crabapple trees that looked like where the elk had gone.

Yellow Hair waited patiently watching the trail and all around the cluster of crabapple trees. He held his new man's bow proudly. He saw Strong Wing making his way toward the crabapple thicket from his right, his route was shielded from the crabapple thicket by a low hill. Yellow Hair caught a second movement following a distance behind Strong Wing. There were three men wearing clothes unfamiliar to Yellow Hair, but they fit the description of the enemy, Minquas, he had heard about. All three had strung bows and nocked arrows. They were obviously stalking Strong Wing.

Yellow Hair nocked his own bow and worked his way behind the three men. He caught up to them just as Strong Wing flushed the elk from the crabapple thicket. The big animal thundered toward the place where Yellow Hair had been hiding. Strong Wing watched the elk charge, unimpeded, past where Yellow Hair was supposed to be. Frustrated, Strong Wing threw up his arms.

At that moment, the first warrior drew his bow up, aiming his arrow at Strong Wing. Yellow Hair decided instantly that he could not let anything happen to his partner. He quickly drew and released, striking the Minquas warrior in the back. The other two warriors turned to face Yellow Hair while he was nocking his second arrow. As two bows were drawn up, targeting him, Yellow Hair knew he did not have time to get another arrow off, so he dove behind a small cedar. Two arrows cut through the small tree just above his head.

Some primeval survival instinct came over Yellow Hair. He jumped to his feet and charged right at the two warriors while he pulled his war club. They had no time to reload before he was upon them, but they separated enough that Yellow Hair could not fight both at once. He caught the closest one, breaking a blocking arm with a vicious swing of his club. The second man was about to drive his club into Yellow Hair's back when Strong Wing's arrow slammed into the man's exposed armpit, penetrating all the way into his neck. He was dead in a few heartbeats.

The man with the broken arm rallied, swinging his club at Yellow Hair with his healthy arm, who was quick enough to duck, and drive his own club hard into the warrior's knee. The warrior went down screaming in pain. Yellow Hair bent down and grabbed the man's club from his good hand. The man looked up and realized he had been beaten by a very young, very strange-looking warrior. The wounded warrior's look was one of incredulity. Yellow Hair smiled at the man's disbelieving eyes.

"What will you do with this one?" Strong Wing asked as he walked up beside Yellow Hair.

Yellow Hair looked around, saw the two dead men, and began shaking, realizing he had just killed a man. "Wha-wha-what are th-they d-doing h-here?" he stuttered.

"I would say they were scouts, trying to determine Sun Town's strength. They saw me, thought they had an easy kill, and came after me. I guess they won't make that mistake again. Then you somehow appeared and ambushed them. I saw you dive behind that cedar. When you came out yelling and swinging your club, they were in shock. That gave me enough time to nock and aim an arrow at that one." Strong Wing pointed to the one he killed.

Yellow Hair saw his captive draw his knife and slammed his club down on the warrior's wrist. He could hear bones crack under the force of his club. The man screamed something in his own tongue and tried to kick Yellow Hair with his good leg. Strong Wing slammed his club into the man's head, ending the struggle.

"That answers the question about what to do with him," Strong Wing said, smiling devilishly. "Gather their weapons and take scalps," Strong Wing instructed. "You can have this one. You crippled him—I only finished him off, as a favor. You fought very well for your first time, by the way," Strong Wing complimented Yellow Hair.

Yellow Hair looked at the carnage, turned, and his stomach involuntarily emptied. "I...I...I..." he stammered, shaking like an aspen in the wind. *These enemy warriors are much older than me and probably better fighters. I just caught them by surprise, and luck was on my side.*

"The first time is always hard. But you have amazing instinct and skill. You were so fast, those two did not know what hit them! Come on, let us get this finished and get back to the village. Everyone will want to know that Minquas are scouting these forests," Strong Wing said while pointing to their victims. They took their grisly trophies and left the bodies for scavengers.

That night in a special War Council meeting, Painted Turtle had Yellow Hair and Strong Wing recount their experience with the enemy scouts.

"When their scouts do not return, they will send more to find out what happened to those three. We will need to be more vigilant than ever," Painted Turtle addressed the War Council.

Wolf Chaser, War Chief of the Wolf People, and all of Sun Town rose, stood next to Painted Turtle and held his hand out for the Talking Stick. The intricately carved and painted staff had been used for three generations in Sun Town. Whoever held the Talking Stick could address the assembly without interruption.

"This threat from the Minquas must be handled quickly and with strength. They, no doubt, are tired of fighting among themselves and are testing us for weakness. These young warriors did the right thing in killing them all. The Great Sakimaxkwe's words are true. We must be more vigilant than ever. I will increase the scouting patrols to our north and west in the coming days. With the Great Sakimaxkwe's permission, I will send a runner to Mud Town to inform them of this incident and see if they have been troubled or have seen any new activities to their north," Wolf Chaser stated before handing the Talking Stick back to Painted Turtle.

"Yes, War Chief, I was going to suggest the same things. Until we are sure of what our enemies are up to, all our hunting and foraging parties will stay south of Sun Town. It may put a strain on our winter meat supplies, but I think we can manage," Painted Turtle announced.

———

"MUD TOWN REPORTED that they had, indeed, encountered more Minquas scouting parties, and more than one trader had reported that the River

Nation of the enemy was getting more pressure from the Long Lake and Mountain Nations to move south," Wolf Chaser said to Painted Turtle. "It was reported that the River People have a new, young war chief who is bold and fearless. His name is Ganeco, and he plans to take Mud Town and the West Branch of the Mud River either through negotiations or by force. The traders say he does not have the strength in the coming sun cycle for an all-out war, but he is cunning and ruthless. Sakimaxkwe Sweet Water is concerned for the security of Mud Town."

"The first snow has fallen. It is unlikely this new war chief will take any action now. In the spring, we will need to help Sweet Water defend Mud Town. She controls our northern trade routes to the Monongahela Villages and the Spirit Water River. We must keep Mud Town safe if we can," Painted Turtle replied, her brow wrinkled with concentration.

CHAPTER 22
TROUBLES IN MUD TOWN

Another entire sun cycle passed with only a few small skirmishes between the Minquas and Mud Town hunters. Sun Town did not have any encounters with their northern enemies. Still, Wolf Chaser and Painted Turtle kept Sun Town on high alert, spending extra time training their warriors, making weapons, and generally preparing for a war they knew was coming.

In that sun cycle, Painted Turtle witnessed a transformation in Yellow Hair she did not expect. First, his feet and hands grew to proportions she had rarely seen. During the summer of his fifteenth sun cycle, his body grew far beyond her expectations. By the Gamwing, he was the tallest person in Sun Town. He won many of the wrestling matches and strength contests for his age group. Though not the fastest runner, he outperformed the rest in strength contests and the use of weapons, even though some of his actions seemed ungainly because he had gotten so tall in such a short period of time.

War Chief Wolf Chaser advised Painted Turtle that Yellow Hair was as good as any seasoned warrior and far better than the ones his own age. He could see potential in the young man becoming a great war leader. Painted Turtle was uncomfortable with that. The words of Wild Crow haunted her, *Power has plans for Yellow Hair that we cannot guess and are powerless to change.*

It will be difficult for me to let him go, but I think joining our warriors in a battle against the Minquas is not why the gods have brought him to us. No, I will only let Wolf Chaser use him as a scout in the safest part of any war plans.

———

ON A COLD WINTER NIGHT, Painted Turtle summoned Yellow Hair to her chamber to speak in private.

"You have adapted well to life among our people. I am extremely proud of you, Yellow Hair. Wolf Chaser claims you are among our best warriors and thinks you are suited to become a great war leader. Do you think you were brought to us to become a great war leader among our people?" she asked.

"No, Grandmother, I do not think I am suited to be a war leader. I have this feeling that things will change soon, and I will no longer live among your people, though I will always call this long-house my home. You have taught me much, that I cannot deny. But some feeling deep inside tells me my time here is limited. I cannot explain it," he replied honestly.

"Many your age are already married. Some are fathers. I could, and maybe should, arrange a marriage for you. But I have noticed that you take little interest in our young maidens. Do you find them repulsive? Or is it this 'feeling' that you will not be here much longer?" Painted Turtle inquired.

"I most definitely do not find the Sun Town maidens repulsive, Grandmother. I just have a feeling that the time is not right. In my homeland, our religion dictates that we take one wife to cherish our whole life. Not being able to stay here and be a real husband is on my mind. It would not be fair to the woman or me. Do you understand?"

"You are wise beyond your years, Yellow Hair. I appreciate your honesty.

"Soon the Minquas will be on the war trail, and

I suspect their target will be Mud Town. I have a feeling it will be a bloody and expensive war. For the same reasons we have discussed, I will not have Wolf Chaser depend on you as a fighter. He can use you as a scout, but not in the main part of the war. I want you to remain alive and safe so that you will be whole and healthy when the gods call you away. Do you understand my words?" Painted Turtle pinned Yellow Hair with hard eyes.

"While my ears hear your words, my heart tells me I should be there with Strong Wing and the others when the fighting begins. But I will do as you say. It is not my place to question your leadership," Yellow Hair replied solemnly.

"I will truly miss you when you are called," she said softly, eyes becoming glassy.

———

"We must send help to our friends in Mud Town," Wolf Chaser stated emphatically. "They have been our friends and allies since our people came to these forests. Sweet Water dutifully pays tribute for our help in protecting Mud Town from the Minquas. We have no choice, and we must discourage those cannibal worms from moving south into our hunting grounds. Only Mud Town stands in their way, and they can only resist for so long before they become weakened and overrun. I implore the War Council to send warriors to help Mud Town repel the invasion. This is what I have to say." Wolf Chaser, War Chief of Sun Town, spoke from his place among the Wolf Clan members. He passed the Talking Stick back to Painted Turtle.

"We have heard compelling reasons to go to the defense of Mud Town, and we have heard compelling reasons why we should keep all our warriors here to defend ourselves if Mud Town falls. It is time to make our choice. An open palm means stay here to defend Sun Town, and a tight fist means we send warriors to Mud Town. Raise your hands and let your vote be counted," Painted Turtle ordered.

The overwhelming majority of the raised arms held a clenched fist. "The men of Sun Town have voted to walk the trail of war to repel the Minquas from the Original People's lands. Do the clan matrons wish to say something on this matter?" Painted Turtle turned to the clan matrons of Sun Town. Without prompting, they all raised a fist.

She stated loud and clear, "The Turtle People of the Original People recognize the threat from the Minquas and that this threat must be thwarted. The women of all the clans in Sun Town will provide food for the warriors to carry on this war walk and will anxiously await their victorious return."

The crowded plaza broke out in war whoops and drumbeats. Soon the warriors were dancing. Within days, over ten tens of Sun Town warriors would be on their way to help Mud Town.

———

YELLOW HAIR WAS CAMPED with four other warriors scouting along the West Branch of the Mud River that flowed south and east from the lands occupied by the Minquas. They had raided down that river toward Mud Town all last summer and word had reached Mud Town during the Awakening Moon that the Minquas planned an all-out invasion when the spring flooding had receded. The Minquas plans were delayed by an unusually cold spring with late heavy snowfalls. The resulting flooding delayed corn planting along all the rivers. Finally, the floods receded and the time for war was upon them.

Yellow Hair was on his watch in the middle of the night when he heard a twig break close by. The night was overcast with a light, cold mist drifting through the trees. There was absolutely no light. *Is it my relief? A deer or some other animal? I see and smell nothing.* As he turned his head to squint into the darkness behind him, hoping Wolf Hair was coming to relieve him, a sharp pain intruded from the back of his head just before his world turned black.

CHAPTER 23
ESCAPE

Yellow Hair awoke sometime after the sun had risen. A light mist was still drifting down from a leaden sky. He was under a deerskin blanket and trussed up like a hog ready for slaughter. Pain hammered his head. He could hear the murmuring of low voices nearby but could not comprehend their foreign words. He tried to move but found he was only able to wiggle slightly. His head was covered so that he could only see a small patch of last summer's desiccated leaves in front of his face. He was dreadfully thirsty and sore. Brazenly he said out loud, "I need some water!"

He heard someone rise and walk toward him. The blanket was pulled back from his face, and he felt the cool mist caressing his warm cheek. The face that looked down at him was younger than his own.

Angry words were spoken by another young man who Yellow Hair could not see. He did not understand what was being said, but it did not sound good.

"Ganeco says we are to keep him alive and comfortable until he gets here. You know his tongue, talk to him," the younger man said. Yellow Hair understood the name Ganeco. He was the Minquas War Chief causing all the trouble. He knew if he was still there when Ganeco arrived, he would be tortured until he told everything he knew about the Lenape positions, then killed.

A third voice, from one a little older, spoke up. It sounded like he gave a command. Then the one who sounded angry said in Lenape, "What do you need, you foreign maggot?" His voice sounded hateful, but at least Yellow Hair could understand the words.

"I could really use a drink, but I must make water," Yellow Hair said calmly. A plan had entered his throbbing head.

"Then piss yourself, I do not care. You will get a ration of water later," the hateful voice replied. The older man asked a question in the Minquas tongue, and the hateful voice replied. Then the older one gave a command that sounded threatening.

"It seems you got your way, worm!" said the hateful voice. He then said something to the younger one, who pulled the deer hide clear and went to Yellow Hair's feet to untie the bindings that were tightly wrapped around his knees and ankles, then up to his hands behind his back. In the meantime, the boy with the hateful voice drew an arrow, nocked it in his bow, and pointed it at Yellow Hair's chest. "Just do not do anything stupid," he warned.

With the help of the younger one, Yellow Hair got to his feet. *Now I must find an opening to run. There are four of them. I could overpower the young one who has a spear at my back, but that older one with the arrow pointed at my chest is a problem.* They were on a southwest facing slope. Just to the east was a small valley that ran down to the western branch of the Mud River. To the east of that was a deeper gully with a running creek. He could hear water trickling over the rocks. When he was captured, they were about four days upstream from Mud Town searching for the advanced party of Minquas warriors.

The two guards guided him to the low in the bottom of the shallow valley. The youngest one was stationed behind him with a spear at his back.

The other was just uphill and off to the side. The young one untied his hands so he could tend to his business, but then came around, so that he was almost in front and held his spear close to Yellow Hair's belly. A slight thrust would impale him.

Yellow Hair saw his chance. In a flash, he grabbed the spear and pulled the young man between him and the older guard just as he released his arrow. As Yellow Hair planned, the arrow went through the young man and stuck out the side toward him. He held the boy up with one hand and took the spear in the other. When he dropped the boy, his other hand wrapped around the spear shaft and drew back. He stepped forward and threw it with all he had at the older guard who had just started to draw his second arrow back. The spear drove into the warrior's chest just as the guard started to let out a whoop. Yellow Hair scrambled to him, picked up the bow and loose arrow, nocked it, and released just as the third guard came over the hill with his bow drawn. Before the man could pick out his aiming point, Yellow Hair's arrow sliced through his throat. He dropped his bow and reached for his neck as blood bubbled out of the hole around Yellow Hair's shaft. The fourth guard topped the hill, saw what was happening, dropped his spear, shrugged off his bow and quiver, and ran as fast as he could to the northwest.

Yellow Hair quickly grabbed two waterskins, a bag with pemmican and some other items, a spear, the bow he had used, and an antler-handled flint knife that the older guard had in his waist belt. He also gathered every arrow that would fit in the quiver he took and dashed off to the east. When he topped the hill between the little valley and the one with the running creek, he saw a small cave opening on the hillside several paces away. He carefully made his way to the creek and then walked on rocks in the water so he would leave no tracks. The mist was still falling, so he could not help leaving tracks from where the fight took place.

He made it up to the cave and squeezed through the entrance, then found it opened up into a larger room where he had space to move just a bit. He could smell fox urine. Maybe she would come back and offer him a meal—that is, if the Minquas did not find him first. He was able to maneuver a rock that had broken off from the ceiling to the front of the opening. It was big and heavy enough that it would be difficult to move from the outside and could not be pulled through the opening. He could defend the opening one man at a time with the spear he took.

He finally relaxed and assessed his options. If he moved off to the north, he would be heading into enemy lands, and he did not relish that idea. In fact, there were Minquas in every direction he went from here. No choices were good. He finally decided that he would wait for dark and then move out to the east. If he went far enough, he would intercept the Lenape River and make his way back to Sun Town. It would take many days.

He took a bite of the pemmican and drank some water. A hard rain came through that washed his muddy tracks away from the cave entrance. After the rain passed, the clouds disappeared, and the afternoon turned sunny. He could see that it was about midafternoon.

He started to hear strange noises, like human voices, but not normal ones. His first thought was that he was dreaming of witches, then realized he was wide awake. As the sounds grew stronger, he could tell it was running feet, many of them. Or rather, shuffling feet. Finally, he caught a glimpse of warriors running north up the slope a bit to the west. They were Minquas, and they were fleeing uphill as fast as they could. A closer look revealed that they were young warriors, mere boys, like two of those who had been guarding him. Several were wounded and were struggling along. The unhurt ones were helping many of the injured ones. One was shouting what sounded like orders, maybe trying to hurry them along. They passed by far enough away that none noticed the dead guards or the little camp where the guards had held him. Soon enough, their sounds faded as they topped the hill and worked their way northwest.

In a short while, more noises came from down along the river and running men—many more of them—began to appear. One bunch of them came up toward where his prisoner campsite was. Someone was yelling, as if expecting an answer. As they got closer, Yellow Hair could see that many of them were wounded as well. The Lenape must have handed them a defeat. It seemed that more than half of them were hurt. Even with help, some were barely able to move along.

An uninjured man who must have been looking for him and his guards arrived at the campsite. He yelled out, "Ayieeeeeeee!" Another man yelled back and hobbled on a wounded leg toward him. The first warrior looked around and saw the guard who had been shot in the throat. The dead man's body had contorted, arching his back when he died into an unnaturally gruesome position. Even from his position in the cave, Yellow Hair could see a large amount of blood around the body. With the sun came clouds of flies to lap up the blood. The warrior next found the guard

Yellow Hair had killed with the spear and finally the boy who was still skewered by his friend's arrow. The man dropped to one knee and caressed the boy's forehead.

Yellow Hair surmised the man was the boy's father or uncle. He probably assigned him guard duty thinking it was safer than going into battle. The man looked around at the tracks and assessed what had happened. About then, another man arrived. He, too, was not wounded. That one yelled something to the one over the dead boy, and they shouted back and forth a few moments. The man with the boy looked around. His gaze came right at Yellow Hair, then moved on. He looked defeated as he broke off the arrow shaft and picked the boy up over his shoulder, then moved on up the hill with his companions. He never looked back while in Yellow Hair's sight.

By the time the noise of the retreating warriors died away, the sun was setting over the western hills. He decided to try to get some sleep before moving out. If he left now and went running downriver toward the Lenape, he might be taken as an enemy and killed. If he waited until morning, he risked the Minquas planning another attack and being caught in the middle. He decided to sneak out in the night and try to make his way east to friendlier territory.

He traveled only a few hours each night, finding a rock enclosure, a big deadfall, or hollow tree to hole up in for the daylight hours. During the second day, he heard Minquas warriors moving back south before sunrise, but they were far enough away that he was not afraid of being found. Later that day, they were shuttling their wounded back north. After the fifth day, he no longer heard any more human sounds.

When he ran out of pemmican, he was able to find a few old nuts and roots that were edible. Still no ripe nuts from the current season, but he did discover some that squirrels had cached and forgotten. He managed to club a couple of unsuspecting grouse and shot a turkey. He decided not to shoot any deer since he could not use much of it. He had an encounter with a mountain lion but managed to scare it off by acting aggressively without shouting. He was surprised he met no hunters. Painted Turtle must be sending all of them south to avoid contact with the Minquas.

———

YELLOW HAIR's fitful sleep was interrupted by a blood-curdling, ear-piercing scream. His eyes popped open to see a barn owl right in front of him, perched on the same limb less than two body lengths away. The owl looked right at him. Yellow Hair was perched four man-heights above the ground in a sprawling, ancient chestnut tree in a clearing. He could see a long distance in every direction and still remain hidden on his perch. *What are you doing this deep into the woods, my friend, and why are you looking at me and not flying away?* An overcast sky kept the sunlight from appearing too bright, but that did not answer why a night creature was here this late into the morning.

The owl turned his head in the direction Yellow Hair had come from last evening. The animal moved his head in circles and flared the feathers around his heart-shaped face as if concentrating on some sound, unknown to Yellow Hair, on his back trail. As he studied the direction of the owl's attention, he detected movement. *Trying to warn me, friend?* He turned to find the owl gone. No sound of flight told him the owl had left. *Was it a dream? Spirit helper—an owl? Not likely.* He turned back to study his back trail. He could see now there was one man, too far away to identify. But the man was assuredly following Yellow Hair's obscure tracks.

I can climb down and run...and be caught in a hand of time. Or I can take a chance that he will miss my trail to this tree and wait for him to go away. Or I can ambush him from here when he gets close enough if he does not see me. If he does see me, he will just wait me out until I run out of water. I think he will be in range before he realizes I am up here. I will wait.

A hand of time passed before he could identify the man as an enemy. *He looks familiar—he is the man who cried when he found the dead boy where I escaped! He has been hunting me for days! I hate to kill a loving father, but I have no choice.* He slowly nocked an arrow.

The man found a broken twig in a small depression a hundred paces from Yellow Hair's tree. He studied it then looked for another and found one. He was feeling the bed of leaves for a moccasin-shaped depression less than fifty paces away when Yellow Hair's arrow drove into his shoulder at the base of his neck. Yellow Hair climbed down and walked over to the man cautiously, an arrow drawn. The man's eyes blinked in pain as he watched Yellow Hair approach. Too much blood oozed from the wound. Yellow Hair knew the stranger would not live long. "Are there others?" he signed. The man tried to say something, but his throat was choked with blood. He only made a hoarse gurgling noise. His body went limp as he expired.

Yellow Hair took up the man's bow, which was much better than the one he had taken from the guard. He unstrung the old one, stuck it between two close-growing tree trunks and snapped it in two. He added his three remaining arrows to the ten and four the man had been carrying in a much better quiver. Then he retrieved the man's war club from his belt and found a fine obsidian knife hafted to a section of deer antler. Finally, he grabbed the man's waterskin and shoulder bag that contained pemmican, a fire kit, and a spirit pouch. He left the spirit pouch with the man, thanked him for his weapons, and was on his way.

CHAPTER 24

TRAVELER IN SUN TOWN

Two canoes slid into the Sun Town landing in the early evening after five long days on the fast-moving river. Four canoes full of young men had escorted them for the last hand of time before they landed. "Curious lack of canoes at the landing. And few men here to greet us," Bear Claw noted to Traveler.

"Yes, it appears we have arrived too late. The warriors have already left on their war walk," Traveler said with frustration in his voice.

"Hoo, Bear Claw, grandfather to young Petal here!" shouted a lithe young woman from the crowd of women and children who were gathered at the landing.

"Willow Branch, my heart sings to see you and Petal!" Bear Claw shouted back as he stepped out of his canoe. He reached down, picked up the toddler and held her up. "You are growing faster than a snow lily in early spring, little one." She giggled at the attention from a man she did not recognize. He set her back on the ground and reached into a bag he had slung over his shoulder. He pulled out a beautifully painted tiny turtle-shell rattle and handed it to the child. She took it, shook it once, then put it in her mouth as everyone around her laughed.

"Come, let us move up to the Sakimaxkwe's lodge. You can introduce your friend there," Willow Branch said enthusiastically to Bear Claw. She ordered several of the older boys to carry the trader's packs up to the Turtle Clan lodge and to pull the canoes up onto dry ground.

Once in the presence of Painted Turtle, Bear Claw proceeded with formal introductions. "I remember this trader from long past," Painted Turtle said as she touched a shell gorget that hung from her neck. Traveler had brought it from Cahokia and had bargained with Painted Turtle's grandfather who gifted it to her grandmother, the Great Sakimaxkwe at the time.

"It looks lovely hanging around your neck, Head Matron," Traveler complimented her. "Your grandmother was a great leader and looking around, it seems that you have taken up her mantle. My compliments." He bowed slightly to her.

"Your silver tongue fits you, trader," she smiled. "Unfortunately, I have no husband for you to trade for another gift for me." She hoped her mirth was evident. Traveler smiled back, thinking correctly that it was an invitation to her bed.

He is a charmer! Bear Claw thought to himself, a slight smile on his face. "We have heard about the trouble with the Minquas, Great Sakimaxkwe. How bad is it?"

"We sent more than ten tens of warriors to help Mud Town crush their raiding parties, once and for all. They should be returning before the Planting Moon so that we can get on with our lives. They have been coming into Mud Town's lands ever since that Thunder Throat became War Chief of the Monongahela Black Bear Village over on the Spirit Water River. Word has it that he is a fierce one, and the Minquas have stopped trying to defeat him, so their attention is turned toward our lands. Sweet Water and Otter have their hands full trying to keep them at bay. We decided to make a show of force to let them know that Lenape People are not to be dallied with," she replied emphatically.

"I have heard of this Thunder Throat. It seems his reputation runs far and wide," Traveler noted.

Have I sentenced Cass to death? The question behind his eyes was not lost on Painted Turtle, but she kept it to herself. She would question him about his concerns in private.

"I am sorry you missed Strong Wing, Bear Claw. He would have liked to see you before leaving on this war walk. You will be happy to know that your daughter-in-law is carrying her second child from his seed," she smiled at him.

He looked to Willow Branch, who looked like a new woman who had just walked out of the women's lodge after her first moon. *How could she be pregnant? She is too thin.* Now he could see the glow in her face as she smiled back at him. "Maybe this time Strong Wing will give you a grandson," she beamed.

"This is good news. I cannot wait to tell Red Feather. She will want to come to see you. The Summer Solstice Celebration in Sun Town this cycle will be a particularly joyous one!" Bear Claw's joy overflowed, the thought of his son off at war forgotten for the moment.

"There is the matter of the Minquas to tend to first, War Chief," Painted Turtle interjected.

"Yes, Great Sakimaxkwe. Do you need more warriors? I could probably send three tens and still keep the southern alliance from attacking Willet

Village," Bear Claw offered, returning to the serious war talk.

"I do not know, War Chief. I am expecting a runner with a report from Mud Town any time now. If you can stay a few days, we should hear how things are going," she replied. She turned to Traveler. "So, do you have many marvelous things from Cahokia for us to look at?"

"Yes, I have some very interesting things for your eyes only, and something private to discuss with you, Head Matron," Traveler answered. Everyone in attendance was stunned by Traveler's forwardness. Even Willow Branch's mouth dropped open.

"A bit forward, aren't you, trader?" Painted Turtle snapped. "What makes you think I would just grant you a private audience just at your lewd suggestion?"

"I need to talk to you privately, but it has nothing to do with a lewd liaison, Matron Painted Turtle. It is purely business, or maybe even political in nature. But it must be between just the two of us," Traveler said seriously as he looked directly into her eyes. "Preferably, we would walk out by the canoe landing where our talk will reach no one else's ears."

"I will grant you that, mysterious one. But

guards will be posted where they can watch us," she retorted.

"I have no problem with guards as long as they are outside of hearing range and Bear Claw is one of them," Traveler answered resolutely.

"So long as it does not take too long. I do not wish to keep Bear Claw from talking with his daughter-in-law. I am sure they have much to say to each other," she challenged.

"The length of the discussion will depend on you. Willow Branch and Petal can join Bear Claw at his guard position—there will be no trouble," he said calmly.

"Can we get it over before the evening meal?" she asked.

"That is up to you, Matron," he answered quickly.

CHAPTER 25

TRAVELER'S GIFTS

T raveler offered Painted Turtle a seat on Bear Claw's overturned canoe. "It has come to my attention, Matron, that you are in possession of a certain yellow-haired boy. Is that true?"

"No. I am 'in possession,' as you call it, of no such thing. There is a yellow-haired young man whom we have adopted into the Turtle Clan who lives among us. Why do you ask?" Her reply betrayed shock and mistrust. *So, the gods send this wily trader to wrest Yellow Hair from us. I was hoping this day would never come.*

"According to a dreamer in Cahokia, this stranger was sent to you by the sky gods to learn the honorable ways of the Original People. He is to be brought to Cahokia where he is to counsel the

Great Sun. It is believed he is a messenger from the sky gods to help the Great Sun in the planning and governing of Cahokia as the city evolves into the greatest center of human activity in the world," he explained. "The task of bringing him to Cahokia has been given to me. It was presumed that your people had taken him as a slave, so I have brought some great treasures for payment," he explained. *I can tell I must be honest and open with this one—she is too perceptive to hide the truth from her. Most attractive, as well,* he observed.

"That story sounds preposterous. When he came to us, he was but a boy. He has grown big and strong in his time with us. We believe him to say he has seen ten and five summers. But he is as tall as our tallest man and his shoulders are broader. His muscles ripple, and his skills with weapons are unmatched. He learned many fighting skills before he washed up on that beach. But he bleeds and feels pain like any young man.

"I can tell you he has a great yearning to get back to his own people, but he has no idea how. He says he was lost at sea for about two moons and only an accident brought him here. He talks about a single god who controls all men. That this god lives in a place called Heaven that is located somewhere beyond the sky.

"He easily passed every initiation test," Painted

Turtle continued. "Our shaman and elders determined that the trials he survived while lost on the Great Ocean had surpassed any tests that we may have given him. Once, more than a sun cycle after he arrived here, he killed two Minquas while defending a friend. He is ready for your Great Sun, but he is no god himself.

"He is a fine young man and has many maidens standing in line to marry him. But he is more interested in destroying the Minquas threat and naturally went on the war walk with our other warriors. I gave instructions to our war chief to use him as a runner or a scout. That yellow hair of his makes him an easy target no matter how good he is with his war club." She felt like she was saying too much.

"Then I should wait until he returns and talk directly to him? He is a free man?" Traveler asked.

"We certainly do not wish to see him leave our town, but technically, yes, he is free to choose his own destiny, as any warrior is. I do not think he fully understands clan duties and responsibilities. I have our spirit leader, Wild Crow, working on that.

"Where he comes from, men own everything, including the land! Who ever heard of such a thing? How can a man own land? Supposedly when a man dies the land passes on to his oldest son. If he has no son, it goes to his daughter, who gives it to her husband. Preposterous! We are working on educating him." She smiled and shook her head. Obviously, the foreigner had touched her heart.

"So, what treasures have you brought to bribe me into breaking my clan laws and turning Yellow Hair over to you?" she asked with a wry chuckle.

"I have heard that you named him Yellow Hair. Does he accept that name? Bear Claw said the custom among his people is that a person is given a name at birth, or quite young, and that name is given to their god to know that person by. Once that name is given to their god, there is no changing it—another strange custom they have. Although I will admit that Traveler is the only name I have ever known. It was given to me by the couple who found me in the days before I could even talk, and it has stuck through all the sun cycles. Of course, I had no clan and have not had to live by clan rules..." Traveler trailed off.

"He did not argue with his naming. Sometimes he has a distant look in his eyes, like he is waiting for something to happen. Possibly, your arrival here is the sign he is waiting for," she said, looking away. A wetness appeared in her eyes. "I have lost two husbands and a son in my life, trader. All good men. I hate to lose another good man if you get what I am saying?" She wiped the tear that trickled down her cheek with her doeskin sleeve.

"Yes, it seems too many good people are taken from us before we are ready to let them go in this life," he said quietly, putting a comforting hand on her shoulder. "Perhaps we should return to your lodge now. We can talk about treasures another time." She nodded and stood up.

———

"I EXPECTED you to be wearing some fine new broach or gorget by now, Mother," Round Shell sniped at her mother. "If he is going to be sharing your bed, you should at least get something for it. After all, he is just a lowly trader—he has nothing but trinkets to offer. You are worth more than any trinket he has, anyway. Why do you put up with him?"

"Enough! Traveler and I have an under-standing of sorts. He is here for something I do not, and cannot, possess, but that does not mean we should ignore what we can give each other. I know it is only a temporary arrangement. But it is a good one for now. The details you do not need to know. Just trust me to have my own life," Painted Turtle tersely addressed her daughter.

"You are the Great Sakimaxkwe, you can do as

you please. Bed a weasel if you like. Just do not be surprised when it bites you," Round Shell said bitterly.

"I hope your insight improves before something happens to me. May the gods help Sun Town if I die before you grow up." With that, Painted Turtle got up and walked out into the bright sunny morning.

As she approached the canoe landing, she noted Traveler bent over his canoe. Hearing Petal laugh, she looked back toward the pahsaheman field and saw Bear Claw bouncing along with Petal on his back, giggling with joy. Willow Branch stood nearby talking with some friends. They were all smiling and laughing, with children lined up to ride on the big man's shoulders. *That is the future of our clan!* She smiled to herself.

She wandered down to Traveler, thinking he was merely cleaning tree catkins from his canoe. When she got close, she saw the false floorboards that had been removed, and indeed, there were treasures laid out on a white deer skin. He picked up a gorget made of a circular seashell the size of the palm of his big hand. Painted on it was a detailed picture of an eagle-man soaring across a blue-sky background. Without acknowledging her presence behind him, he said, "I thought you might appreciate this." He turned around and handed it to her.

"It is beautiful!" she said. "Surely it must be worth a field of harvested corn. I cannot accept such a valuable gift just for keeping your blankets warm while you are here."

"Look closely," he said. "It is to always remind you of the time you had with Yellow Hair."

She looked closely, and sure enough, the eagle-man had an eagle's beak on a man's face that was the color of Yellow Hair's flesh. The eyes were bright blue, and yellow hair flowed past the shoulders as if blowing in the wind while flying. In place of arms were broad eagle wings. A manlike torso with eagle-like legs folded in the manner of a flying eagle ended in yellow-scaled feet with black talons. A golden eagle's tail stretched out behind the flying figure. "Such detail. It is amazing."

"It was painted by the dreamer who envisioned Yellow Hair's arrival on the beach by Willet Village and role in the future of Cahokia," he noted.

"I cannot believe he could make such a likeness without ever seeing the young man," she said, her voice filled with awe.

"I have learned that there is a lot more to life than living from day to day. You never know what the gods are going to throw at you. After all, our lives are limited...short if you will. But the gods, or spirits—call them what you wish—never die. They are always around, watching us, bending us to their will. I did not always think that way, but more and more, I have come to believe it." His voice was solemn.

"You are a wise man, Traveler. I find it hard to believe some woman, somewhere along your travels has not pinned you down and made you a chief." She searched his eyes for a hint of vulnerability and saw none.

"There you go again, trying to hang responsibility on me. It just does not fit," he quipped.

"No? This quest covering half of the world to find a single person and drag him back to your precious Cahokia is not a responsible act? And caring about the feelings of the people you meet along the way? Who do you think you are fooling? You are as responsible as any man I have ever met. You are just afraid to admit it because you do not want to be tied to one place, one clan, one woman. That does not make you irresponsible, just noncommittal. There is a difference. I, for one, hope you never change. Just keep doing good things wherever you find yourself." Her voice reflected her sincerity.

He briefly envisioned Corn Stalk while she talked. "Here, I want you to give this copper turtle broach to Round Shell. Maybe it will make her feel better about my 'trinkets' and her feelings." He smiled conspiratorially.

"A prize for every damaged soul?" she asked slyly.

"Something like that. Coming from you, it will be better than coming from me," he said knowingly.

CHAPTER 26

MUD TOWN
WAR NEWS

T he days passed. The women prepared the ground and planted the corn in clusters along rows in each clan's designated fields. When the corn emerged, beans, squash, and pumpkins were planted so that the beans would climb the corn stalks while the squash and pumpkins would shade the ground around the corn clusters to save moisture and slow weed growth. After planting, days were spent hoeing unwanted plants from around the emerging crops. The days grew longer and warmer while the three crops grew rapidly, watered with frequent rains.

————

THE PEOPLE of Sun Town waited anxiously for word from their warriors sent to defend Mud Town. Late in the Moon of Planting Corn, five canoes came downriver. A whoop arose to alert the townspeople that warriors were returning. It was a small party, with two healthy paddlers and five wounded men in each canoe.

"What news of the war, Red Lance?" Painted Turtle asked their leader as the canoes slid onto the landing. "Get these wounded men tended to," she ordered the women who had run to the landing.

"Great Sakimaxkwe, the war goes well, but the Minquas are a persistent rabble. Their losses are great, but they keep coming back to fight. A captured worm testicle says they are being pushed south by their brethren, the Long Lake People. I fear they will not quit until they push the Original People from the Mud River valley. Having said that, I think they are nearly ready to give up fighting until after the corn harvest. Their losses are far greater than ours. Only five Sun Town warriors and less than a handful from Mud Town have been killed, and most of these wounded warriors will be ready to rejoin the fight in the fall," Red Lance reported rapidly.

"There is something you are not telling me,

Red Lance. What is it?" she asked, her eyes boring into his soul.

"Great Sakimaxkwe, I know he lived in your lodge, so he was important to you, but the foreigner, Yellow Hair, has disappeared." He looked at his feet while relating the news.

"Disappeared? What does that mean?" she demanded.

"He was with a party of scouts watching our northern flanks. One night he was on guard while the others slept. When his relief went to take his place, he was gone. His bow and quiver were left leaning against the tree where he had been standing, and his war club lay on the ground a few steps away. There were four sets of enemy tracks but none of his filing back to the north. The scouts started following the tracks. One set was digging in deeper, like Yellow Hair was being carried. Now and then a drop of blood lay on the trail.

"Soon they began to see the main force of the enemy approaching, so they had to retreat to warn the rest of us. We met and drove them back to the north that day, but no one has seen Yellow Hair since. We have questioned every warrior we have captured, but they claim to know nothing. I fear that by now, Yellow Hair has been tortured and probably killed. If they were going to ransom him, they would have sent word by this time. He has been missing for more than a moon. The rest of the Sun Town and Mud Town warriors are defending Mud Town. As I said, it appears the enemy has given up fighting for the summer moons but will probably be back in the fall," Red Lance related solemnly.

Painted Turtled listened intently, pain written on her face. For the first time since he arrived, Traveler noticed the age lines around her mouth and eyes. She was more attached to the yellow-haired stranger than she ever let on.

———

"THE MINQUAS SAY they are ending their war on Mud Town until after the corn harvest at the end of summer. They hold a Green Corn Celebration somewhat like ours. Given that, I would expect them to attack after that. This could mean that they are weakened right now and need time to heal before resuming the fighting. But it could also be a trap. They may be trying to lure us into attacking them on their terms in their lands. I would recommend we do not make that mistake," War Chief Wolf Chaser of Sun Town spoke before the special combined Sun Town and Mud Town War Council.

"Your words hold wisdom, War Chief. It pains

me that three of our young warriors were captured. No doubt they suffered great torture before their deaths, but there is nothing we can do to help them now," Painted Turtle said, her eyes looking past the Council members.

"Perhaps we could send a smaller war party to test their strength, then decide a course of action, Great Sakimaxkwe Painted Turtle," Bear Tooth, War Chief of Mud Town, suggested. "It seems unlikely they would kill the Sun Town scout, Yellow Hair. He is a foreigner. They would either try to bend him to their way of thinking, and may have, or ransom him back to us. A small party may even be able to get in and rescue him, then escape."

Traveler stood up and went to the center of the Council room. He took the Talking Stick when Bear Tooth reluctantly offered it. "I am a foreigner here but was invited to listen and perhaps offer a suggestion or two by the Head Matron, Painted Turtle. It is evident that the fate of Yellow Hair and the other captives is unknown. While it..."

"Why are we listening to this trader?" Kills a Bear, Second War Chief of Mud Town interrupted. "He has no stake in this, no matter what we decide. Why should we take counsel from him?" Several heads nodded in agreement, and loud murmuring ensued.

"Quiet!" Painted Turtle shouted. "We are in Sun Town's Council Lodge, and I am Sakimaxkwe. I invited Traveler here to speak because he has seen many things and is wise beyond his station. He holds the Talking Stick and will not be interrupted. You might learn something!" she stated emphatically. "Traveler, you may proceed."

All eyes returned to Traveler. "As I was saying, the strength of the Minquas is unknown. The only way to know is to get eyes into their main village, the village of their war chief, Ganeco. All of you are familiar to the enemy. You could not just walk in there, ask a few questions and leave. But a trader like me could paddle right into his village, make some trades, learn some secrets, and leave. They have never laid eyes on me and would have no reason to be suspicious. I could portage from the Mud River over to the Spirit Water and take that up and portage over to the Gorge River. They would see me coming from the west and not link me with Mud Town. I can gather the information you need to conduct your war, and they will not be any wiser."

"Why would you risk your life and your reputation as a trader to help us? Does that not go against the 'power of trade' you traders are so quick to point out?" Kills a Bear demanded.

"Your concern is well-founded, but I also have

a stake in all of this. Yellow Hair is important to me. I must speak with him. Until I know for sure he is dead, I plan to do that," Traveler replied.

"If he is alive, what makes you think they will let you talk to him?" Sweet Water, Head Matron of Mud Town asked.

"I will not seek to talk to him there. I will just find out how you can rescue him. I will talk to him when he is safely back in Sun Town."

"I repeat! Why are we listening to this trader? I say we attack the worm bellies and take our chances that the foreigner still lives. If not, at least we cripple Ganeco to the point he is unable to fight us again," Kills a Bear said emphatically.

Otter, husband of Sweet Water stood, took up the Talking Stick, and faced the Council. "We have heard war talk, and it sounds inviting. But we have also heard an alternative that comes from wisdom. The trader's words are true, and his plan is sound. I met this trader many sun cycles past. He gave me some advice then that gave my soul a partner in this life who I would have walked away from had Traveler not swayed my mind with his wisdom. I trust him and know that his words are bedded in truth. I say we send the trader into the land of the Minquas to learn what he can of their strength and the fate of our lost warriors." Everyone except Kills a Bear expressed agreement with Otter.

Five days later, Traveler and the Council members were on the Mud River moving toward Mud Town. Bear Claw accompanied Traveler and would wait for him in Mud Town until he returned from Ganeco's village. The eight-day trip was interrupted and delayed one day by a storm that brought heavy rain and powerful lightning.

———

BEAR TOOTH, War Chief of Mud Town, looked at Traveler across the small campfire and asked, "Traveler, do you recall those many sun cycles past, when last you were in Mud Town, a young boy running around named Grasshopper?"

Traveler looked closely and saw the resemblance to Sweet Water. "Ah, yes! You were always bouncing around with your friends, looking for mischief as I recall. I do not think I saw you still once while I was in Mud Town back then. Now you are a grown man with great responsibility. You are the brother of Sakimaxkwe Sweet Water, are you not?"

"Yes, she is my sister. You came at a bad time in her life, but after you left, Otter came around courting her, and they have been happy ever since. She tells me you were responsible for getting them back together after the warrior who hurt her was outcast. My family thanks you for that effort," Bear Tooth said sincerely.

————

ONCE IN MUD TOWN, Traveler wasted no time preparing for his search into Minquas lands for the missing Yellow Hair. He had chert and obsidian blanks, knives, arrowheads, scrapers, and spear points. He also had bundles of chokecherry arrow shafts, some copper rods, and several deer, beaver, and mink skins. Sweet Water donated some decorated clay pots. He left his finest Cahokian artworks and western shells behind because he was aware Ganeco was more interested in weapons than artwork. He also had taken the false floor out of his canoe, thinking a man like Ganeco might figure it out and tear the craft apart.

CHAPTER 27

TRAVELER AND GANECO

Ten days later, Traveler launched his canoe into the Gorge River and started north into Minquas territory. The river was shallow, rocky, and fast-moving. It was difficult maneuvering his big birch bark canoe down the treacherous channel. Within a day, a canoe with five fierce-looking warriors joined him. He held up his white staff indicating he was a trader and signed "friend." They motioned for him to proceed. That night they made camp together.

The first thing Traveler noted was that four of the five bore healing wounds, probably from the earlier fighting near Mud Town. "I have willow tea and herbs to help with healing wounds," he said in his best eastern dialect, Haudenosaunee tongue.

"Nightshade better...forget pain," said the

oldest of the warriors. These northern people spoke in a tongue Traveler had little experience with, but he understood the man. He had not thought about packing nightshade and had to admit that he had none. He put in a very restless night, not knowing the intent of these warriors. Each man moaned in his sleep. Obviously, their wounds were not healed yet.

The next day they arrived at a large, randomly scattered grouping of wigwams and tents next to the river. Some women were busy hoeing around newly sprouted corn, bean, and squash clusters on the flatter ground between stumps. The smaller trees had been cut down to build the shelters. There was no broad floodplain here, but the corn looked healthy. Others were scraping deer skins, pounding corn in wood mortars with log pestles, tending fires, sewing clothes, or serving wounded men tea and gruel.

More than half of the men wore blood-stained bandages over some part of their bodies. A good many were inside the wigwams, too injured to come out to watch the stranger come up from the canoe landing. Traveler quickly surmised that this was a temporary village recently thrown together in haste. There were no longhouses, which understood these people normally inhabited. He expected that they decided this was a safe place to stop and heal their wounded rather than continuing the rest of the way to their more permanent village if they had one.

In the center of the cluster was the largest wigwam, adorned with a life-size wood carving of a wolf's head over the door hanging. A young boy ran to that wigwam when Traveler first came up the path from the canoe landing. A man wearing only a breechclout stepped out. His face, arms, and chest were heavily tattooed with wolves, spirit wolf-men, and geometric patterns of dots, triangles, spirals, and other small designs. He had a single roach high on the back of his otherwise shaved and tattooed head that hung in a braid halfway down his back. His expression was grave. Traveler guessed the man had not yet seen three tens of summers. He looked Traveler over with disdain. "What brings a trader to Ganeco's village from the west? No trader has come up the Ohi-yo River for many sun cycles. How did you get past Black Bear Village?" he snarled.

"Great Chief, it appears you have been in some terrible fighting. I have heard no news of your plight, or I would not have disturbed you. My name is Traveler, and I have traded my way up the Spirit River and the Ohi-yo. Black Bear Village, as you say, was unfriendly and the trading was poor there. The war chief and few matrons that were allowed to meet me wanted me gone as quickly as possible and would not permit me to return down-river. They never said as much, but I suspect they wanted me to run into trouble. There were no organized villages until I got here. Perhaps I have some goods that will help your cause." He hoped between his signs and his broken Haudenosaunee, he got his meaning across.

"You are a clever one." Ganeco smiled. He admired someone witty enough to get past Thunder Throat. "Let us see what you have before I decide if you are to live."

Traveler signaled to the warriors who had carried his goods up from the river to spread them out on the ground near the central fire pit. By now, every person who was able to walk had gathered around the trader and their chief.

"Get the trader some tea," Ganeco ordered a downcast-appearing woman. Her big breasts and stomach bulge told Traveler that she was with child, and the patterns on her worn and dirty dress said she was from a Lenape village. He wondered how many captured slaves lived here.

Traveler bent down and opened a pack that had tanned deer skins in it. He spread four of them out on the ground, then proceeded to lay out the trade goods from the other packs. He got lots of "oohs" and nods as he spread the colored chert and obsidian pieces out. The arrow shafts and turkey feathers were well received as well. The women were interested in the beaver pelts and the clay pots.

"Traveler, you have some fine things here. It puzzles me that Thunder Throat allowed you to go from his village with this many weapon goods. I have seen many traders in my time, but never have I seen one with more items of war in one trader's canoe. Thunder Throat does not like having weapons anywhere except in his possession. Tell me again how he let you go." It was not a question from Ganeco.

"People downriver told me he was not friendly. I had my canoe packed in a way that I did not have to show these weapon goods. I only showed the pelts and pots, and some chert scrapers, things of a domestic nature. I had some decorated shell gorgets. He did take those and the few chert blanks I let him see in exchange for my life. I regret to say that he took all of them, so I have no pretty shells for you to give your woman." He nodded to the woman who had brought him the tea. She looked at the ground.

"Where did you come by these sticks of copper?" Ganeco asked. Traveler was impressed that these people deferred completely to their chief. Ganeco had done all the talking.

"They were formed by copper workers in Cahokia on the Grandfather River, Great Chief. Traders from far north in the headwaters of the Grandfather River bring rocks with the copper embedded in them. The craftsmen heat the rocks over hot coals until the copper melts out and drips into long hollowed and wet Cyprus limbs. When it cools, the copper can then be worked into these long, thin rods that are a good way to transport them for trade. The copper rods can be pounded and worked into any shape a craftsman wishes to make," Traveler explained.

"I like many of the goods you have here, Traveler. And you seem to know many things. Let us sit and share some talk and drink. Then I will decide what to do with you," Ganeco said matter-of-factly.

Ganeco and Traveler sat on reed mats, and the woman brought more tea. The chief asked, "Where are you going, trader? To the north and west, there is war with the Mountain and Roaring Waters Peoples; to the east, the Long Lakes People are fighting with everyone. To the south, Mud Town is at war with us and will not welcome you coming from here. Thunder Throat will certainly kill you if you show up back there. So where will you go?"

"My plan was to get to the Great Eastern Ocean to trade for some exotic seashells and pottery. I had planned to go down the Mud River but found myself on the Gorge River instead. I have not been this way before and did not know the Gorge River and Mud River looked so much alike in the headwaters. I reckon I will go back that way and hope that they honor the power of trade in Mud Town," Traveler answered nonchalantly.

"Heh, heh, heh," Ganeco replied. He thought for a moment. "This 'power of trade' you talk about. You traders think highly of that power. But as a war chief, I must take other things into consideration. Tell me, trader. How strong is Black Bear Village? Thunder Throat has had a stranglehold on the Ohi-yo River for seven sun cycles now. Is his power diminishing, or is his town flourishing?"

"I do not know that I can answer you fully, War Chief. I was not invited to go into the palisade. What little business we did was outside the village walls. I can say there appeared to be several healthy warriors. Few women appeared to my eyes, as most stayed inside the walls, I expect. There were a few working in fields. There seemed to be the normal number of children with their mothers and a handful of young women working along with the older ones. They were not close, but they looked healthy. The sound of mortars thudding reverberated from the enclosure, and several trails of smoke climbed into the sky. It seems they were in fairly good shape," Traveler answered, lying as best he could. He hoped his broken language would help with his ruse. The talk continued for a hand of time. Ganeco mostly asked questions of a strategic nature, as expected.

Finally, Traveler got brave enough to ask, "War Chief, have you ever heard stories of yellow-haired men who have hairy faces and travel in great winged canoes across the Great Eastern Ocean?"

"I have heard that story from a trader. He said they came to our lands far in the east several sun cycles past. They had evil in their hearts and our people, or some other people in the area, drove them away. But all of that took place in lands that take more than one and a half sun cycles to travel to. Why do you ask?" Ganeco asked cautiously.

"The story reached the Grandfather River and sounded too preposterous. I just wanted to see if it was true. I have never heard of a yellow-haired man before. I have encountered a young shaman who had white hair, but never yellow. Obviously, they never have come to these lands," Traveler scoffed at the idea.

"Odd you should mention that. A scout fitting that description, who had come from Sun Town to help Mud Town repel our invasion, was captured by my men," Ganeco said bitterly.

"Really?" Traveler sounded astonished. "Does he still live? Would it be possible for me to look at him?" he asked with wonder in his voice.

"We have no idea if he lives. He escaped the fools guarding him, killing three of the four in the process. We lost his trail and had to tend to our wounded, so we did not have time to pursue him. Trust me, if I ever get my hands on him, he will know the meaning of pain. One of the guards he killed was the son of one my second war chiefs. He will find the slug turd and bring him back to me." Ganeco's voice echoed his hate.

"Perhaps a bear or wolves will find him first. Surely he cannot know the land and will make a mistake." Traveler sounded as supportive as he could.

"I thought I could get information from him regarding the strength of Mud Town and Sun Town in exchange for escorting him to the coast where his brethren had shown up and might return. Surely he would rather be with them than among those vile, turd-eating mud people south of here. But he ruined any chance he had. Now he will die a slow death," Ganeco promised.

"And well he should, Chief," Traveler agreed. *So, Yellow Hair is running around, lost in the woods someplace with a deadly warrior tracking him. He truly is being tested by the gods.*

"I have decided what to do with you, trader," Ganeco said calmly. "You are good with your tongue. You will go back upriver, then to the Mud River. Wolf Killer will show you to the Mud River. Once you get to Mud Town, you will convince Otter to come back here, with you, to negotiate a peace between Mud Town and the Real People. In doing so, you will note how many warriors they have and their fighting ability. When you return with Otter and give me the information I seek, you can have your canoe back and some of your trade goods and go where you wish. I will keep the weapon materials. Our trade is completed. You and Wolf Killer will leave at first light."

CHAPTER 28
TRAVELER RETURNS

"You are back in one piece!" Bear Claw greeted Traveler at the landing outside Mud Town.

"As expected, Ganeco is a hard man. I must talk to Otter and Sweet Water. Where are they?" Traveler asked solemnly.

"They left yesterday for Sun Town. The Solstice Celebration must go on, even though most of the warriors are compelled to stay behind to defend the town from Ganeco." Bear Claw replied in a frustrated voice. "Do you have any news of Yellow Hair?"

"Yes. It seems there is more to him than a polite young man. Ganeco told me he escaped his guards, killing three of the four, and disappeared. Then he said he has an experienced warrior out hunting him. He will bring Yellow Hair back and torture him to death for killing his guards. I must report what I have found as soon as possible to Painted Turtle and Sweet Water!

"Ganeco said he had planned to get information from Yellow Hair regarding Mud Town and Sun Town's strength. After he learned all Yellow Hair had to say, he would have had him escorted to lands far away to the north and east where people of Yellow Hair's tribe come to trade from time to time. He would be reunited with his own kind. But that all changed when Yellow Hair killed his guards, including the son of a second war chief," Traveler explained while they prepared a canoe to depart for Sun Town.

"If he knew what Ganeco was planning, he might have cooperated," Bear Claw mused. "Where do you believe he went? He should have been able to walk back to Sun Town by now. Surely somebody would have seen him with so many traveling to Sun Town for the Solstice Celebration."

"That is why we need to get there—so we can let everyone know he is out there somewhere. Remember, he has a killer tracking him. If he knows it, he is being careful. If he does not know, it is probably too late. We need to get there as quickly as we can. Are you ready?" Traveler was anxious.

"What about the things you left in Ganeco's village? Do you not want them back?" Bear Claw asked eagerly.

"When I do not show up with Otter in a few days, my things will be distributed. and Ganeco will probably own my canoe. No, those things are forfeit," Traveler replied resolutely.

"You are a good man, Traveler. I am sure Painted Turtle will make sure you are back in the trade business before you leave Sun Town. She seems to have taken a liking to you, as have other women, I have noticed." A wry smile appeared on Bear Claw's face, but Traveler, as he was busy climbing into the back of the canoe, did not see it.

Five hard days and little sleep later, they could see smoke rising from campfires along the river north of Sun Town. "Fresh venison stew today!" exclaimed Bear Claw. "The Solstice Celebration starts tomorrow. There will be black drink, and I will share a blanket with Red Feather!"

And I will have to tell Painted Turtle that Yellow Hair is out in the forest somewhere all alone...or dead. Traveler frowned as he looked off to the west side of the river. Coming down a sparse hillside was a figure carrying what appeared to be three turkeys.

His curiosity made him look closer until he realized the hunter had a head full of yellow hair.

"Look!" he yelled to Bear Claw. He could barely contain his excitement.

Bear Claw glanced over his shoulder, then looked to where Traveler was pointing. "In the name of the gods, it cannot be," he said, dumbfounded.

CHAPTER 29
YELLOW HAIR RETURNS

It had taken a little less than two moons from the time Yellow Hair managed to escape his captors before he finally saw the smoke rising above Sun Town's palisade and along the riverbank. Activity along the river told him the Summer Solstice Celebration would go on.

He sat on a rock overlooking the town across the river and contemplated his choices. It was near midmorning. The air was warm, with a slight southwesterly breeze, and just a few puffy white clouds appeared in the sky. *The Original People surely think I was captured, probably tortured and killed by now. The Minquas probably assume I made it back to Mud Town and still want to seek revenge for my escape. Norsemen are in Greenland, wherever that is—probably far to the north and east of here. I have heard the northern regions are peopled in some places by relatives of the Lenape and other areas controlled by the warlike relatives of the Minquas. It would be nearly impossible to travel only at night and go undetected all the way to lands friendly to the Norsemen. People are gathering for the summer solstice at Sun Town. Maybe I will see Bear Claw and some others from Willet Village.* He made his decision to go back to Sun Town and look for an opportunity to find his countrymen another time.

Just then another movement caught his eye to his left. He slowly turned to look and saw at least a dozen turkeys picking through last year's acorns on the ground beneath a spreading red oak tree. *If I am going back, I should bring some meat,* he thought as he carefully laid out four arrows. He slowly drew back his "new" bow and let the arrow fly into the closest turkey. The rest of the turkeys were confused by the dying bird's commotion, and he got off two more shots before the other birds escaped over the hill and out of range. Three turkeys would make a good present to Painted Turtle. After gutting the birds, he tied the turkeys' feet together with a buckskin thong he found in his stolen shoulder bag, then slung two over his back and let the other lay against his chest. He unstrung his bow and walked triumphantly toward Sun Town.

————

WHILE TRAVELER and Bear Claw were straining to keep their eyes on Yellow Hair as he walked toward the river's west bank, they were oblivious to the shouting from the east side where Willet Villagers were camped.

From far away, Bear Claw heard his name being called out. Slowly it dawned on him that the sound was closer than he thought. Finally, he looked around to see Red Feather standing in knee-deep water, yelling at him as they drifted by. "I think we better paddle back upstream and land on the east riverbank," he said.

"Why? Yellow Hair will come to the west bank, and we can give him a ride across to the main canoe landing," Traveler said, still looking to the west bank where Yellow Hair was no longer visible because of the steep riverbank.

"Because we just passed right in front of the Willet Village campsite, and if we do not go back, I will be divorced before we make it to the west bank!" Bear Claw exclaimed.

"Oh, sorry," Traveler muttered, still trying to look over his shoulder at the west bank while Bear Claw powered the canoe back up to the Willet Village camp.

When they slid to a stop, Bear Claw climbed

out, and Red Feather threw herself into his arms. She jumped up on him and wrapped her legs around him to hold herself in place while she planted a big kiss on his lips. "You look amazing!" she exclaimed. "Do you know how I have missed you? Were you in on the fighting?" She looked him over for signs of wounds.

"No, everything turned out alright. I cannot say more until we talk to the Great Sakimaxkwe. Did your parents come?" he answered.

"Yes. They said their old bones would not be able to withstand the portages, so we carried them. They are guests in the Great Sakimaxkwe's longhouse, and we are to go there as soon as camp is set up." She swung her arm to indicate Bright-Eyed Boy and Little Star, who saw their father for the first time in two moons and ran down the bank, into the water, and clung to him.

"Bright-Eyed Boy, you are nearly a man!" Bear Claw said to his ten-summers-old son.

"I have killed ten and two rabbits and a fox this summer, War Chief," his son replied formally.

"You catch up with your family. I am going to meet Yellow Hair," Traveler called as he back paddled the canoe into the river. Just as he arrived at the west bank, the yellow hair of the young hunter came into view.

"Greetings, Yellow Hair," Traveler said, startling him. He did not expect a stranger to know his name.

"Do I know you?" Yellow Hair asked as he set the turkeys down on the bare dirt riverbank, relieved to get the weight off his tired body, and placed a hand on his pilfered war club.

"I am Traveler, a trader from Cahokia. I have come a long way and waited a long time to find you," Traveler said seriously.

"I am Yellow Hair, and I will talk to you sometime, but first I must see the Great Sakimaxkwe," Yellow Hair answered.

"Yes, I am on my way to see her myself. Jump in, and we will be at the palisade quickly," Traveler said enthusiastically.

"I do not know whether to accept your offer or club you to death. It has been a while since I have met a friendly soul," Yellow Hair said. For some reason, he already liked this trader.

―――――

"You found him! I knew my faith in you was well-founded," Painted Turtle exclaimed, smiling from ear to ear and a tear trickling down her cheek. Round Shell looked away and shook her head in disbelief.

"You better get the whole story from him

before you give me any credit. Then I will tell my story," Traveler replied. He looked around and saw Sweet Water and Otter standing by the fire pit.

"Get these weary travelers some tea and venison stew," Painted Turtle told her young female attendant. "Come, Yellow Hair. I have missed you more than words can tell. We feared we had lost you to the Minquas."

"I must go see what the children are up to." Round Shell got up and walked out of the longhouse. Everyone just looked at her quizzically. No further explanation was given, but Traveler rightly guessed that Round Shell was jealous of the attention given Yellow Hair by Painted Turtle.

Yellow Hair detailed everything that had happened to him from the time the war party left Sun Town until this morning when he killed the three turkeys, which by now had been added to the stew pots lining the fire pit. Those in attendance were astounded with Yellow Hair's escape story.

Next, Traveler detailed his visit to Ganeco's camp. Otter perked up when he heard the part where he was supposed to return to Ganeco's war camp to negotiate a peace. Traveler noted the look in his eyes. "You are right, Otter. Had you gone back there with me, I do not believe either of us would have walked out again."

"And what do we do now?" Sweet Water asked with concern written on her face.

"There are always options, Sakimaxkwe Sweet Water," Wolf Chaser answered. "One is to prepare for a short, frantic fight in the fall. Ganeco will certainly make good on his promise to attack after their Green Corn Ceremony, which we combine with Gamwing here in Sun Town. Second, you could attack him in his weakened state. But the time for that is probably passed. Third, to be out of this war climate altogether, you could think about moving Mud Town further from the Minquas lands. There are acceptable town sites further down along the Mud River, and certainly good sites are still available on the Lenape River. Think about how much easier it would be for us to come to your aid if you were on the same river."

"All your suggestions are valuable, as usual, War Chief. Our Council will take these things into consideration before making a decision," Sweet Water replied formally.

Traveler could not contain himself. "Matron, I must submit to you that as War Chief Wolf Chaser has suggested, that his second option is not a sound one. I had the feeling that Ganeco was showing his wounded men to anyone coming down the Gorge River purposefully. A man like him is full of tricks. And he certainly was not going to reveal any of his real strength or plans to me. I think an invasion into his lands would be a trap that you would regret."

"There is no question that there is truth in your words, trader. But I must ask, what is your stake in all of this? You are a trader from far away and will soon be gone from here. Why do you care what takes place so far from your homeland?" Wolf Chaser asked.

"I know that Sweet Water and Otter are fine people, and I would hate to see anything bad happen to them. Just as I would be filled with remorse if anything terrible happened among any of my Lenape friends, War Chief. If I can stop someone from making a mistake, I find it difficult to keep my mouth shut. I apologize for stepping on anyone's toes," Traveler answered matter-of-factly.

CHAPTER 30
STINGER

On the third day of the Solstice Celebration, the final pahsaheman game was played between the Sun Town men and the Round Track Village women. Strong Wing scored three times, and Yellow Hair scored twice. As the contest wore on, the Round Track women proved to be up to the challenge. Eventually, the score was tied at eleven sticks each.

Yellow Hair lined up as the elder was about to toss the ball straight up. By this time, the deerskin ball stuffed with deer hair had become tattered and out of shape, making things a bit more unpredictable. Lined up across from Yellow Hair was a fierce-looking young woman named Stinger. She got that name from being stung by a bumblebee whose stinger became embedded in her cheek. The wound was invaded by demons and became pus-filled. At last, the shaman was able to drive out the demons and remove the unusually large stinger. Everyone started teasing her by calling her "Stinger," and the name stuck. A small scar remained on her cheek, as if to confirm her name.

Stinger had scored four times. She was athletic and clever. When the ball was tossed, Yellow Hair and Stinger went after it hard. Their collision was violent, leaving them sprawled out on the ground. Yellow Hair had a bloodied and broken nose, and Stinger's eyebrow was cut. Blood flowed down her face, and it looked as if she was trying to regain her bearings. Yellow Hair got up and staggered aimlessly, holding his painful nose. Both finally remembered they were in a game and staggered after another woman who was carrying the ball. The girl tried to toss the ball to Stinger as Strong Wing and another young warrior went after her. Yellow Hair stepped in front, jumped, and stopped the ball in mid flight. By the rules, he had to stand and kick the ball to a teammate. As he was lining up to kick the ball to Strong Wing, Stinger barreled into his side, knocking him down. She ended up on top of him, the cut over her eyebrow dripping blood onto his cheek.

She said in a near whisper, "Meet me after the game on the riverbank by the Round Track campsite." Then she got up and chased after the ball. Just as Strong Wing was about to kick it, she swooped in, grabbed the ball off the ground, and ran all the way to the women's goal to score the winning point.

Yellow Hair was still on his knees trying to regain his composure when Stinger scored the winning point. He found himself thinking more about her pretty face and feminine body than losing the game.

After the game, he and his teammates went to the river and washed the blood and smeared paint from their bruised and battered bodies. But no one was tired. There was a whole night of dancing ahead. And all the men had young women on their minds. That and the black drink, which would be generously flowing all night, adding to the magic of the final night of the Solstice Celebration.

After Yellow Hair cleaned up and put on the new, highly decorated ceremonial shirt, breech-clout, and moccasins that Painted Turtle had made for him, Painted Turtle gently rubbed some medicinal paste on his sore nose. His eyes were blood-shot; his nose and upper cheeks swollen. But he was ready to get out there and find Stinger. He secretly regretted washing her blood from his face and chest.

The sun was beyond the western hills before

he found himself walking along the riverbank just outside the Round Track campsite. He frantically searched for Stinger among the people milling around. Dejected, he decided either she had been only teasing, or he was too late. Surely others would be after her too. He was about to turn around and wander over to the main fire pit where the dancing was now getting underway, and the black drink was being served.

Suddenly, there she was. She had on a form-fitting, dark tanned doeskin dress with long fringe around the bottom hem. It was sleeveless, but long fringe hung from the arm openings. The shoulders were sparsely decorated in geometric patterns with colored porcupine quills. The dress accented her shapely body. A large, shell wolf track was embroidered on the chest. Her long hair was pulled back and held in place with bone combs and a wide buckskin headband sparsely decorated with porcupine quillwork. The band also held a mink skin bandage soaked in willow bark mixed with bear grease over her wounded eyebrow. The wound had been closed with sinew stitches. The eye was swollen half-shut, and the skin around her cheek and eye was red, obviously bruised. Her arms were splotched with new bruises and a few scratches. She was beautiful.

"You look a sight, young warrior," she said,

indicating his wounded face with an abbreviated painful half-smile.

"I only see the most beautiful woman in the world." He was surprised at the words that came out of his mouth. She blushed and continued to smile, then quickly said, "Warrior, your eyes must be very damaged. I stand before you bruised and wounded. I am anything but beautiful."

"We can talk about that later. Would you like to go to the dances?" he came back, more logical than he expected.

"Yes, but first I want to spend some time getting to know you. This is my first time at a summer solstice outside of Round Track Village. My family has never been able to come before. Forgive me—I have heard about you from others, but here at this Celebration is the first time I have seen you. Please tell me about yourself, like where you came from. How you came among the Original People. That sort of thing."

"The same questions I hear everywhere I go. I am but a curiosity, no more. I am not one of your people, so I am not a *real* person. I wish I could find my way back to the fatherland," he answered dejectedly.

"Please, I did not mean to insult you. I am sorry. Tell me about your home," she said apologetically.

She listened slack-jawed, as he described Norway and shipbuilding. She put her hand on his shoulder compassionately as he described the harrowing voyage through the storms, losing his family, crew, and ship, and finally washing up on the beach four sun cycles past. He described his capture and escape from the Minquas. "You are the bravest man who ever lived!" she said with awe in her voice. "You should be talking with a Matron's daughter, not a mere planter."

"What are you talking about?" he asked exasperatedly.

"You are above my low status. You will be married to a Sakimaxkwe one day, not a planter like me," she said humbly.

"You must understand better than me. I have no clan. I am not one of the Original People. I have no status. I am nobody—just a curiosity. Even if I did find my way back home, I would still be a nobody. I have lost all my family. No one knows or cares about me any longer. I am all alone." He said it as if he were in the confessional in Father James's church in Ulfrstadt.

"You must have been brought to this place for a reason. I do not believe you are a nobody. You have greatness in your eyes...well, not right now. You just have blood in them right now!" She laughed.

He shook his head and laughed with her. "You

made a mess of me! For a stupid ball!" He laughed out loud. He had learned that if he talked slowly and quietly, his voice sounded almost normal, despite his swollen nose and cheeks. But when he raised his voice, it came out as a pitched nasal twang. He felt his cheeks burning, but it was too dark to see how red they were.

"Yes, and thanks to you"—she indicated her eye and the bruises on her arms—"I am the most beautiful woman in the world!" They laughed as their faces drew together.

After a passionate kiss, Yellow Hair said, "Well, that was painful." He pointed to his swollen nose as he spoke.

She slid her hand down across his soft shirt to his waist belt and said, "I hope other parts of your body are not as sore as your nose."

He could only half smile. Then he took her hand and said, "Are you ready for the dance now?" She beamed, and they walked toward the fire pit where the dancers were getting into it now.

Exhausted, Yellow Hair left the circle of male dancers and came to stand by Stinger on wobbly legs. She held his ceremonial shirt folded over her bruised arm. The drums continued to boom, but there were not as many as there had been a hand of time earlier. She sidled up close to him in the shadows, slid her hand down his bare, sweaty chest, over the waist ties, and onto his soft breech-clout and said in a husky voice "Are you ready to know me now?"

He could feel the blood rush to his throbbing nose and cheeks, but especially into his growing manhood. "Ah...are you sure it is a good idea?" he asked, losing his composure. Still panting from the vigorous dancing, his voice came out in a nasal twang.

"I am," she said as she led him away from the crowd and around the stockade of Sun Town until she found a small thicket of ash trees. She slipped off her dress, laid it on the ground, and stood before him in the pale moonlight.

I thought she looked good IN that dress! He watched her gracefully pull off her moccasins. Completely naked, she came to him and took his head in her hands and pulled his face to hers, gently kissing his sweaty cheeks, then passionately on his mouth. As she was kissing him, she slowly slid a hand from his face down his neck, over his wide shoulder, and down his back. When her hand reached his breechclout, she found the ties and deftly untied them until the soft tanned skin fell to the ground. Without stopping her kiss, she cupped her hand expertly around his scrotum, then gently gripped his hardened manhood.

He pulled his mouth away from hers and said

in a meek voice, "I have never been with a woman before. I do not know what to do."

She just smiled coyly at him and pulled him down onto her dress next to her. "It is easy to learn," she whispered in his ear. Then she took his hand and placed it on her soft pubis and encouraged him to explore. "Feel what I am like. Learn me with your fingers," she sighed into his ear. As he explored, she became more aggressive. Soon she pulled him on top of her and guided his manhood into her waiting woman hole. As he filled her, she moved her hands to his broad shoulders and slid them down until she gripped his buttocks and pulled him into her. She wrapped her legs tightly around his.

Afraid of crushing her, he propped up on one elbow and gripped her firm breast with the other hand. She moaned her approval. As he pushed himself into her, it seemed her whole body caressed his manhood. She was warm and wet, and squeezed him hard as pleasure swept over them both. It seemed all too soon to him that his release took him. He could not think of any feeling to compare it to. At the same time, her body contracted and convulsed in time with his as she moaned in desperation.

When they began to relax, and he breathlessly slid onto his side next to her, he was reminded how painful his nose was. In the silver moonlight filtering through the trees, he could see smeared blood on her cheek. *Oh no! My nose started bleeding again.*

Feeling the warm moisture on her cheek, she rubbed it into the bittersweet tears oozing from her eyes.

"Did I hurt you?" he asked fearfully when he noticed the tears.

"Oh no, that was anything but painful," she replied. "It's just that...well...this will be the only time we have this. You belong here, and I must go back to Round Track. I will miss you dearly, Yellow Hair. Thank you...for giving me this one time," she said both joyfully and sadly at the same time.

"What if we have made a baby?" he asked quietly.

"We didn't," she said quickly. "My moon will start before we Round Tracks camp on the river tonight. I will tag along in a canoe all by myself, then purify the canoe with cedar smoke after we get home before anyone else can use it."

"What if I want to come along with you?" he asked, knowing the answer.

"No, your place is here, at least for now. You are too young to know who or what you are. But I know this. You are not destined to be a planter's husband. Greatness awaits you, and that could never happen in Round Track Village. I am destined to be a lesser clan matron in a small village. That will not change, and that is too small a place for you," she said quietly.

"None of us can know the future. The time we have spent together has been the best since I landed on that beach. I want more of this." He gently cupped her breast as he talked. "There is a fire between us that can change our circumstances. We can be who we wish!"

"Wrong, Yellow Hair. *You* can be who you wish. I can only be what I am. I am a planter who can play pahsaheman, nothing more. I will return to Round Track, my mother will choose me a new mate, I will marry and have children. My first 'promised' husband was killed by a bear before we were married. One day I will replace my mother as clan matron as she will replace her mother. And one day my daughter will replace me. That is how my life is written," she said with no remorse or sadness in her voice.

"But I was destined to raise sheep in Greenland, and here...I do not know who or what I am. The point is, circumstances can change," he said, trying to make it sound like he knew what he was talking about.

"Do not do this, Yellow Hair. You were obviously chosen by the gods for a special purpose. You cannot change that. You must follow your destiny. Accept that, and you will be happier." She tried to convince herself as much as him. She knew she would never end up with a man who cared about her as much as this foreigner.

"I will never forget you, Stinger. Your name suits you—you have stung my heart," he said sadly, taking his hand from her breast.

She put her hand on his manhood and said, "Light has not yet come to this day. Know me one more time before we part."

———

YELLOW HAIR STOOD on the bank alone and sadly watched the Round Track Village canoes disappear around the bend as they paddled their way north. Stinger was alone in a canoe several paces behind her mother's loaded craft. One final wave, and she was out of his life forever.

"Always hard saying goodbye to a good woman," Traveler startled Yellow Hair. He had not heard the trader walking up to him.

Yellow Hair discreetly wiped his eyes and replied, "I guess you would know. You are always saying goodbye."

"And it never gets easier. But what is, is. I was wondering if I might enlist you in helping me build a new canoe. As you heard, mine was lost to our mutual friend Ganeco. Painted Turtle offered me one of her dugouts, but I prefer a good birch bark craft because they are lighter, and they can hold more if they are made right. Together we could have it done by the Gamwing celebration. Then I will be on my way," Traveler said evenly.

"I think I would like that. I worked in my father's shipworks," Yellow Hair replied.

"Your father's what?"

"*Shipworks*. The place where we build big shi... great canoes." Yellow Hair still had trouble thinking as a Lenape.

"Tomorrow we will go find some trees. Today, I think by the look in your eyes, you need to sleep. Dream of your lost maiden and smile," Traveler suggested, knowing what Yellow Hair and Stinger had been doing all night.

CHAPTER 31
GAMWING IN SUN TOWN

Willet Village arrived at Sun Town. As always, the Sakimaxkwe and her family were invited to the Sun Town Gamwing in honor of the bond made by the marriage of Strong Wing and Willow Branch. Sakimaxkwe Wattle, Long Beard, Red Feather, and Bear Claw, along with their children Bright-Eyed Boy and Little Star were evening-meal guests in Painted Turtle's lodge. Clam Shell was now Soaring Hawk after his passage into manhood. He still wore his hair in a long braid, for he had not yet completed any war deeds or killed a bear.

By midwinter, Willow Branch would deliver their second grandchild. Bear Claw and Red Feather looked forward to that joyous event. Wattle and Long Beard were too feeble to walk far,

so the carrying chairs made for the Solstice Celebration were put to further use. Strong Wing,
Willow Branch, and Petal were also present. Traveler and Yellow Hair were officially invited guests,
even though both were sleeping in Painted Turtle's
longhouse.

When all guests were seated in Painted Turtle's
longhouse, all formal introductions were made,
and the shaman, Wild Crow, asked the Creator for
blessings and puffed sacred smoke in the four
sacred directions, plus the sky and underworld.
Painted Turtle asked Wattle for news from Willet
Village.

"We have had a most bountiful growing
season with timely rains and no destructive
storms. Our granaries are full, and we have
brought more than the asked tribute for your
generous allotment of warriors to help in the
defense of Willet Village," Wattle addressed
Painted Turtle. "We lost no children to sickness or
accidents, and five children were born without
incident. Two others were stillborn, and another
young mother died giving birth to her first child,
who also died. We had seven boys pass their initiation rites into manhood, including Soaring Hawk
here. He and two others have had visions to share
during our Gamwing in midwinter. Before we left,
I had news of three newlywed women who are

with child. One of our clan elders, Bramble of the Hawk Clan, went to live with her ancestors. She was replaced by a cousin, Singing Hawk. We have suffered no warfare or raids from other villages thus far this sun cycle.

"We have received news by way of a trader that the Great Sakimaxkwe in Lenape Town is petitioning her Council to make war on Willet Village to force us into the southern alliance. The same news we have heard from traders," she said scornfully as she looked at Traveler, "for three tens of sun cycles."

She turned to Traveler and spoke in a haughty tone. "It seems unusual to me, trader, that you are still in Sun Town, and even more surprising that you are a guest for the evening meal in the Great Sakimaxkwe's longhouse."

"My circumstances are a long story, Matron," Traveler replied glibly.

Wattle continued, looking at Yellow Hair. "Hoo, Tuh. My heart smiles to see you healthy. We heard that you had been captured by those dreadful Minquas."

"Sakimaxkwe Wattle, his name is Yellow Hair. You know we never use the boy's name after he becomes a man. The boy ceases to exist. I will not have you using a name that no longer applies to him," Painted Turtle said sternly.

"Great Sakimaxkwe, did he not tell you that in his land, names do not change at maturity? That a name, once given, stays with that person for life. I was just respecting his customs, as he has tried so hard to honor ours," Wattle spoke with determination, and maybe a bit of scorn in her voice.

"We asked Yellow Hair his preference before his naming ceremony. He said that he is here, so he will live by our customs. He was given a name that fits a man. And that is that. He has proven himself in battle and had more than one spirit vision during his harrowing voyage across the Great Eastern Ocean, and he has been helped by an animal spirit helper," Painted Turtle spoke emphatically.

"Have they found a wife for you yet, Yellow Hair?" Wattle kept digging.

"Sakimaxkwe Wattle, I will soon be leaving Sun Town with Traveler. I have no immediate plan for return. I could not ask a woman to lose her husband so quickly," Yellow Hair answered respectfully.

"So, the trader was able to meet the Great Saki-maxkwe's price, and you are to become a servant to some chief in Cahokia?" she asked disdainfully.

"It is not like that, Sakimaxkwe Wattle. I am leaving of my own volition, as a free man. I have come to recognize that I am not of the Original

People and must follow the plans the Creator has laid out for me." *I especially have no desire to stay in this place if I cannot have Stinger at my side.*

"It will be most unfortunate if we must fight the Minquas on one end and our own people on the other. The southern alliance is too powerful and corrupt. The spirits must indeed be angry," Painted Turtle stated to change the subject.

The talk went on for another hand of time with Wattle and Painted Turtle sparring over Yellow Hair's feelings. Finally, Painted Turtle declared that the time was late, and everyone should retire to be rested for the start of the Gamwing.

———

ON THE FIRST night of the Gamwing, at a prearranged time, Wild Crow appeared secretly at the west side of the Big House which was filled to overflowing. In addition, more than two hundred people were positioned in rows around the outside of the Big House, straining to hear what was happening inside. Wild Crow danced in from the west door to the beat of a big drum. Once inside, the drum fell silent, but he continued to dance around the room while making a beat on a small turtle-shell rattle. One-half of his body was painted black, the other half red. He wore a black-colored breechclout and an oval-shaped mask that was painted half black and half red, like his body. The mask was a human-spirit face and represented the Creator *Manitou*. It was a smaller version of the large masks fixed to the center post in the middle of the Big House. From a pouch on his waist, he took out a yellow powder and sprinkled it on the fire. The yellow powder hissed when it hit the flames and put out a pungent odor that quickly filled the room. After he circled the room four times, he stopped at the west end of the fire pit. There he stood facing east and yelled, "Hoo!" Designated people in the crowd yelled, "Hoo!" back at him. This was repeated four times.

Next, he recited the creation story, and when finished, he shook the rattle and danced around the room four more times before disappearing out the west door. Once he was gone, the drum started again, and a row of men got up and danced around the fire pit. Others joined until they formed a solid line encircling the center of the room. After they danced four times around, women got up and formed a solid ring of dancers on the outside of the men and danced around in the opposite direction four times. Then, they all danced in the same direction four times, at the end of which, the drumming stopped. Everyone went back to their places. Soon the drum started once more, and the process of dancing repeated. Dances were performed to ensure good hunting, a mild winter, fertility of crops and women, and the health of children. When dawn broke, the dancing ended, and everyone went to sleep except certain women who were charged with preparing hominy and stew.

The process was repeated at sundown the next night without the creation story. On the third night, after the drum started, a man dressed in a bear-skin suit entered from the west door. He made every effort to scare the children as he danced around the fire pit four times. He then selected six designated warriors who he shooed out the east door with him at their heels. They wore their best hunting shirts, leggings, and head-dresses and carried their bows and arrows. They would run through the crowd outside the building, out of the palisade, and into the forest. The hunters would not return until they killed three deer and carried them back for the feast.

After the bear dance, Wild Crow stood in his finest ceremonial buckskins and recited prayers to the Creator, the sky gods, the gods of the under-world, and the four sacred directions. When he was done, he called for a certain elder to come forward. That elder introduced a warrior who stood before the crowd and recited a spiritual vision that he had experienced. When he was finished, another elder introduced another warrior. The vision stories continued until dawn when everyone was sent to their sleeping blankets. The designated women prepared food for the next night's feast.

By midafternoon, the day after they were sent out, the hunters returned with three fat deer. One was hung on a special pole set up a few paces east of the east door of the Big House. There it was ceremoniously skinned and roasted hanging in place. Anyone was welcome to come up and cut pieces of meat from the carcass as it cooked hanging from the pole. The other deer were butchered and added to various stewpots.

The vision stories followed dancing for the next six nights. Yellow Hair was introduced by Wolfmane, a respected warrior of the Wolf Clan of Sun Town, and recited his story of the barn owl coming to his aid in the forest. After his story, Yellow Hair took his place next to Painted Turtle.

Finally, after ten nights, the Gamwing ended. Everyone was exhausted as the visitors broke camp and started back to their home villages. The Willet Villagers stayed an extra day to allow Wattle and Long Beard more time to rest before their journey back to Willet Village. Wolf Chaser led ten canoes with five warriors in each as they escorted

Sweet Water, Otter, and the rest of the contingent from Mud Town back home. It was hoped the presence of Sun Town warriors would deter Ganeco from resuming his war walk.

The Mud Town people came to say their farewells to Yellow Hair and Traveler. Many of the goodbyes with Traveler were tear-filled. At his age, it was unlikely he would be paddling this far from Cahokia again. Bear Claw told him he was all right for a trader. Traveler took that as the highest possible compliment.

———

Four days after the Willet Village people headed downriver, Traveler and Yellow Hair were packed and ready to leave at first light the next day. Painted Turtle had difficulty saying goodbye to both. "The men in my life have a way of disappearing," Painted Turtle said sorrowfully, a tear trickling down her cheek as she held Yellow Hair by the shoulders and looked up into his eyes. "You have grown so much since you first came to stay with us. Are you certain your destiny does not lie with us? You are so strong. Perhaps you were sent to us to fight off the Minquas," she said, her voice shaky.

"I think Traveler is right, Great Sakimaxkwe. My destiny lies in the west. He seems to have a way of knowing these kinds of things. If the future allows it, I will return to your longhouse. I have learned much from you and your people. I would like to say goodbye again to Strong Wing, but another hug for Willow Branch and Petal will suffice. No one has been kinder to me than you, Great Sakimaxkwe Painted Turtle. I will never forget you. And I will always pray to my god for your protection," Yellow Hair answered quietly. With that, he turned and made his way to where Round Shell sat weaving a small mat from reed grasses.

"We were not destined to be friends, Round Shell, but I wish you well in the future. I pray that your husband comes back from the war walk healthy and strong, and that you are able to enjoy your grandchildren for many sun cycles," he said warmly to her.

"Yes, and I hope that you find whatever it is that you are supposed to." She did not get up or say anything more. Both Painted Turtle and Willow Branch looked at Round Shell in disbelief. She kept her eyes on her weaving and did not see the reproving looks she was receiving.

"Petal, I will miss you waking me up in the morning with your loud voice. You are the best waker-upper ever!" Yellow Hair put his hand on the little girl's shoulder. She beamed back at him, then hid her face behind her mother's shoulder. "Do not get up," he said to Willow Branch, kneeling down to embrace her. "Your man will be a great warrior. I pray your family prospers," he told her as he stood back up.

"Your stay here has been all too brief, Yellow Hair. I, like grandmother, wish you would find a reason to stay. I know some young women who wish you would stay as well." She winked at that last sentence.

"Perhaps I will come back to visit them too," he said smiling, knowing it would never happen.

"Your nose is almost as good as new, just a little crooked. That girl from Round Track was more a warrior than a planter, I think," Willow Branch tested him.

"Oh, she was just playing the game as it is supposed to be played, I expect," he quickly said in Stinger's defense. Willow Branch did not push it any further.

Painted Turtle and Traveler said their good-byes in her sleeping blankets. "I don't know whether to wear out that big manhood of yours or stick a bone stiletto through your ribs for leaving me!"

"I think I like the first choice better," he replied cautiously. Their lack of sleep showed in their eyes in the morning.

CHAPTER 32
NEW MUD TOWN

Traveler steered the canoe to the west bank of the Lenape River as the sun settled behind the western hills. "Are you ready for a rest? We have been moving since sunup, and I am in the mood for some roasted venison. If Painted Turtle was kind enough to send it, we should be grateful enough to eat it."

"I have no idea where we are going, so if you say we have time to camp and feel safe building a fire along the river, I am in no position to protest," Yellow Hair replied.

Traveler set to putting up the small tent and making it comfortable while Yellow Hair started a fire and propped their chunk of venison leg on a couple of sticks to cook. By the time Traveler was finished, darkness was settling on their campsite.

Looking up, Yellow Hair noticed a canoe cutting across the river headed right for them. He reached for his bow and quiver. "Hoo, friends!" rang out from the single person in a long trader's dugout.

"Hoo, stranger! Identify yourself before landing that canoe," Yellow Hair said as he raised his drawn bow.

"I am Long Cat, a trader just up from Lenape Town. I saw your bark canoe and thought you must be Traveler, the trader from Cahokia. But your voice and accent I do not recognize. Who might you be?" the man replied.

"Long Cat? More like Polecat!" Traveler called out. "How long has it been since we shared a black drink?"

"Is there anyone you do not know?" Yellow Hair asked in awe of Traveler's connections.

"Come on up here, you fish eater! We have venison!" Traveler yelled to the man who was climbing out of his canoe. The man was accompanied by a big dog that ran in front of him. "Long as I have been at the trade game, I have met many of the other traders. Long Cat is one of the old ones, and you will never know a better man," Traveler said reverently.

"I heard you were plying these waters...and as many matrons as possible. How are you, old friend?" Long Cat said to Traveler jovially. The trader's darker hair told Yellow Hair that Long Cat was younger than Traveler.

Long Cat looked at Yellow Hair and said "Now there is something you do not see every day! A yellow-haired man is mighty rare, indeed. First one I ever have seen. But I have heard much about you, my friend. I hope you are headed upstream with this cargo, Traveler."

"Downstream, actually. We need to make the Youghiogheny before winter gets too hard. Why?" Traveler asked in a way that sounded like he did not care what the answer was.

"I would be looking for a different route west if I were you," Long Cat replied seriously. "The Great Sakimaxkwe in Lenape Town got wind that you are headed her way with a messenger from the gods. She thinks you have deliberately set out to take power away from her, and she is hunting you. Right now, she thinks you have left Sun Town with this messenger and that you are going to try to sneak past her. She has a fleet of ten tens of canoes on the river searching every craft that comes downriver. If you do not show up in a few days, they will start north hunting you. Her canoes will be joined by a fleet of as many from Blue Crab Town.

"The war chief there says you tricked him, and

he is out for your blood as well. I would say downstream is not where you want to be heading. Your dalliance with Painted Turtle might buy you some protection there, but do not go to Lenape Town if you value your hide or that of your light-skinned friend here."

"Sounds serious, Long Cat. Thank you for the information. Let me introduce you to Yellow Hair. He is no god, just a victim of bad luck. I suppose it is possible that he is being steered by the gods for some purpose none of us can know. He has lived through some harrowing times for such a young man but has survived everything thrown at him so far. I suppose we could take the West Branch of the Mud River and get to the Spirit Water that way. But the Minquas and a war chief on the northern Spirit Water have cut off travel through the northern route. If you are going to Sun Town and do not mind the company, we will accompany you."

"I may be crazy, but I am not a fool. No, I will not be seen with you on this river, my friend. I use this river all the time. If certain people think I am traveling in your company, my life is forfeit. I am not old enough to end up on a stake in a plaza and tortured just because I have a criminal friend. Sorry. I heard you were coming downriver, and I wanted to warn you, just as you once did for me. I must get back downriver now, myself, before anyone misses me. May the gods be with you, Traveler. I hope to hear that you simply disappeared from these waters. Good meeting you, Yellow Hair. I hope you find what you are looking for." Long Cat climbed down the bank, got back in his canoe, followed by his dog, and paddled downriver.

———

"You just keep coming back." Painted Turtle shook her head and smiled as Traveler guided the canoe into the landing at Sun Town.

"Yes, well, we found out we are not welcome downriver. Someone told the Great Sakimaxkwe at Lenape Town about Yellow Hair being a messenger from the gods, and the whole southern alliance thinks I have committed some crime against them by keeping him to myself. They feel he has some power they can put to good use. We cannot take the northern route because of the Minquas, so we will chance the portages on some middle route," Traveler answered.

"And you thought you would hole up here for a few days, maybe get another venison quarter as a gift?" She smiled conspiratorially.

"We do not wish to burden you, Great Sakimaxkwe. We just stopped by to pay our respects. We can be on our way immediately," he answered coyly.

"Let us move up to the Turtle Clan longhouse. I have news from Mud Town," she said seriously. She directed some older boys to take their belongings to her longhouse and put his canoe on higher ground.

"A runner from Wolf Chaser came in yesterday and left early this morning. It seems that Ganeco came to Mud Town carrying the white arrow of peace," she started. "The war chief says that he has recovered his losses from last spring's war and has many, many more warriors available to him than Mud Town has, even with Wolf Chaser's Sun Town warriors. He says he is willing to keep his warriors from the trail if the Mud Town people evacuate the town. He says his people need the upper Mud River drainage for hunting as his people are being pushed from the east and west by others. His only choice is to move south. Otter said he did not believe him and wanted to see this great gathering of warriors for himself. Ganeco and Otter were gone only ten days. When he returned, Otter said they could either fight and die or move from the Mud River and live. Ganeco's warriors were just too many—Mud Town could not produce enough arrows to stop them. The Mud Town Council decided to move the whole town to the Lenape River. Ganeco is giving Mud Town until summer solstice to be gone from Mud Town and the Western Branch of the Mud River. A party from Mud Town will be here any day to scout a suitable location."

"This is terrible news," Traveler said as he gazed blankly into the fire.

"Where did he find the new warriors?" Yellow Hair asked.

Painted Turtle replied, "I do not know for sure. The runner says Ganeco has relatives who live far west and northwest of the Roaring Waters. Perhaps they have come to his aid. His own people must still be weak or else he would not wait to attack. Ganeco did say that his warriors would be free to hunt anywhere north of Mud Town during the 'peacetime.'"

"Traveler, I will stay here and help Mud Town rebuild. They will need all the help I can give them," Yellow Hair said solemnly.

"Of course, we will both help in any way we can. But you and I should stay away from Ganeco's eyes. He has old scores to settle with both of us, and I do not think this 'peacetime' applies to us," Traveler replied.

COLD WEATHER DID NOT ARRIVE until after the new town site had been selected, laid out, and partially cleared. New Mud Town would be located about four days upriver from Sun Town and six days south of Round Track Village. The new site was located on a hilltop near the river that would be easier to defend than the old Mud Town site in the river bottom.

Traveler and especially Yellow Hair lent their backs to building longhouses. Seven clan houses would be needed, plus the largest and most centrally located New Mud Town Big House. It and the society houses could wait. The largest longhouse would be for Sweet Water and her family, the Heron Clan of the Turtle People. Some of the framing poles for it had been set in the ground before the first heavy snowfall. But they enjoyed a relatively open early winter after that and were able to work on something most days well into the season.

On those days when he was not involved in construction, Yellow Hair accompanied Strong Wing and a few others hunting deer, turkey, bear, ruffed grouse, and other small game for food, furs, and bear fat.

Snow was falling, ice was lining the stillwater places along the riverbanks, and the days were getting shorter as the first refugees began arriving in Sun Town. The able-bodied ones rested one night, then went upriver to the new town site to work on their new houses. Soon, the younger men and their families were living in temporary wigwams while they worked on the longhouses. The older Mud Town residents stayed as guests in their respective clan longhouses in Sun Town.

Heavy late-winter snowstorms delayed construction some, but an early spring gave the women an opportunity to plant the three sisters among the tree stumps in the newly cleared floodplain along the river. Heavy runoff from the storms brought the riverbank to full but did not spill out into the floodplain. The rich, newly opened soil would produce good crops. By summer solstice, the men were still busy cutting and fitting large sections of ash, elm, basswood, and hickory bark to the frames of longhouses and smaller single-family houses. The palisade wall had been laid out, and a few men were busy cutting logs and placing them in the trench and lashing them to the previously set vertical logs. At pre-planned intervals, bastions were built along the palisade that would hold lookouts and archers.

The men building New Mud Town and the women who had been clearing, planting, and hoeing the new fields welcomed the break from work for the Solstice Celebration. It was Mud

Town's turn in the rotation to host the celebration, but under the circumstances, everyone went upriver to Round Track Village. Yellow Hair satisfied his curiosity when he met Stinger with a baby slung on her chest and another growing in her womb. It saddened him to see old bruises on her face, but she acted happy. Her husband was not the friendly kind, but he played pahsaheman as well as any man. Yellow Hair did not participate in the games.

After the Solstice, work began again in earnest at New Mud Town. They needed to have the town ready for occupation before Gamwing at the end of the harvest.

Traveler and Yellow Hair planned to begin their trek right after Gamwing, making their way to the Juniata River and heading west then, across the passes to smaller creeks, and finally to the Spirit Water. They hoped for a mild winter.

Again, the goodbyes were awkward at both New Mud Town and Sun Town. Strong Wing and another young warrior guided them through a series of creeks and portages that led them to the Juniata River. From its headwaters they would find their way to the Kiskiminetas River and, eventually, the Spirit Water. They would encounter only a few small settlements and single families along the way and expected to be safe from Ganeco's men on that route. "I am quite confident you will be able to use your charms to convince some matron to provide you a guide through the passes to the Spirit Water River," Painted Turtle had said mockingly to Traveler before they departed.

CHAPTER 33
HEADING WEST

It was early winter before Traveler and Yellow Hair stopped at a friendly settlement near the headwaters of the Kiskiminetas River. They had found the Juniata difficult to navigate due to low water, and the many portages involved had delayed their progress. They had made it across the pass to the Kiskiminetas River, but it was getting too cold, and too much ice was forming on the narrow creek.

The people in the small settlement had welcomed them and invited the traders to spend the cold moons in their secure lodges. The little group did not have a name for their homestead and were loosely affiliated with the Monongahela People. They had only four oval-shaped lodges and just one field dedicated to growing the three sisters.

For commerce, they met the few traders who took that route across the mountains and traded the plentiful deer, elk, bear, and other animals they killed for food or protection. The small group was happy to have little contact with the outside world. Traveler and Yellow Hair promised to help all they could in providing meat for the small community.

Over the long journey, Traveler and Yellow Hair had traded nearly every detail of their lives. Yellow Hair found Traveler's life and adventures even more intriguing than his own. It was difficult to understand that Vinland—or "Turtle Island," as Traveler called it—could be so big. And all the different peoples, tongues, and religions was mind-boggling.

The moon of heavy snow provided just what the name implied. A storm dumped enough snow to prevent any thought of travel. After four days of constant snow, it turned bitterly cold, and the traders were forced to stay longer than they wished. But the settlers welcomed their stories and provided shelter and food in exchange.

The bitter cold finally broke just after the equinox. The deep snow disappeared quickly from the hilltops where the land was buffeted with strong south winds. After a few more days, the ice left the river, allowing Traveler and Yellow Hair to resume their journey.

Now their problem was too much water. The small river ran fast and wild from the snowmelt. It took their combined skill to keep the canoe aimed downstream and out of the most violent rapids. They had to take frequent breaks to rest their weary shoulders and aching backs. The portages were many and difficult, but they finally reached a stretch of the river that was easier to navigate.

After several days with stops at every friendly homestead they encountered, the weary voyagers reached a point where the river slowed.

"This river is being backed up by the Spirit Water," Traveler said while they were setting up camp for the night. "Late tomorrow, we should reach the outlet where the Kiskiminetas empties into the Spirit Water. We will camp there before making the last run to Monongahela Village. It is less than a half day from this river to where the Monongahela meets the Spirit Water to form the Spirit River."

"It will be nice to sleep in a longhouse after these last cold nights," Yellow Hair offered.

"Provided we are still welcome in Monongahela Village. If Corn Stalk feels I sentenced her granddaughter to death, she might strap me to a stake in the plaza," Traveler remarked, only half kidding.

"Ah, the shieldmaiden," Yellow Hair quipped.

"Yeah, well, I just hope she's still alive—for both our sake," Traveler retorted.

Yellow Hair let the subject rest but had to admit that he was curious about the strange girl.

Late the next afternoon, when the shadows were already lengthening, Yellow Hair began to hear the turbulence caused by the merging waters. They were approaching the confluence with the Spirit Water.

"The right bank has a small hill suitable for a campsite. It will keep us dry. Notice the flotsam in the middle is breaking up and spreading out. I think the river has crested. That will make tomorrow easier," Traveler told Yellow Hair.

"See that small bend in the bank? Make for that, and we'll get camp set up," Traveler instructed.

"I think we will have company," Yellow Hair said, pointing to two rising columns of gray smoke on the knoll they planned to camp on.

Just then, a short, swarthy warrior stepped out from behind an elm tree and demanded, "Who approaches?" The man's muscular arms held a drawn bow with an arrow aimed at Yellow Hair's chest.

Yellow Hair recognized the Monongahela tongue that Traveler had been teaching him for the past several days.

"We are traders, protected by the power of trade," Traveler spoke out loudly while he held up his white trader's staff.

"What is this all about?" said another warrior appearing beside the short man. Yellow Hair noted this one was taller, handsome, and just as muscular. The taller man had many bearpaw tattoos on his forehead and cheeks. He had a self-important air about him that made him instantly unlikeable. His buckskin outer shirt and leggings were decorated with Hawk Clan symbols, and a wolf-hide shawl was draped over his broad shoulders. The little heat of the afternoon was quickly disappearing, replaced by a cold wind from the northwest.

"Take us to who is in charge of your party, and we will make formal introductions," Traveler told the warriors as he and Yellow Hair stepped from their canoe and pulled it out of the water, onto the sloping ground between willow trees. Four other canoes were behind a screening growth of small white cedars.

"I will give the orders here," the taller warrior replied harshly.

"Good. Order us to your camp and be done with it," Traveler answered.

"Walk slow and keep your hands out where I can see them," the warrior demanded.

Traveler and Yellow Hair each grabbed a bag that held their personal things and sleeping skins. They walked toward the smoke rising from the camp with their arms out to their sides, lances pointed at their backs.

"We have company!" the tall warrior announced just before four tents came into view. A few people were sitting, others standing, around the larger of the two campfires.

"What have we here?" a mature woman spoke out as a man helped her to her feet. Yellow Hair could not tell how she was dressed because she was wrapped in an elk-hide robe.

Before the warrior could answer, Traveler spoke. "Greetings, Matron Night Owl. It is a pleasure seeing you after all the sun cycles that have passed since I was in your presence."

"Who are you? Do I know you?" she inquired, a puzzled look on her face.

"Of course, you were a young maiden the last time I made an appearance in Black Bear Village. I am Traveler, a trader. I am on my way to Cahokia after trading in the east," Traveler replied, taking charge of the conversation.

"Ah, yes, I remember now. You were a boy. Your father gave this gorget to my mother." She pulled a round shell from her robe. Etched and dyed on it was the stylized image of a spider. "Most traders make an appearance every few sun cycles. How long has it been? Two tens and more? Why so long?"

"My business has taken me many places. And, honestly"—Traveler studied each face and was convinced Thunder Throat was not among them— "talk on the rivers is that trading in Black Bear Village is dangerous business, with an unpredictable war chief." He looked for reaction, knowing he may have overplayed his gaming pieces.

She calmly replied, "That situation has recently been resolved. Allow me to introduce my party.

"The gray-haired man is my husband, Red Loon, of the Heron Clan, the woman is Goldeneye, matron of the Heron Clan. This man is Ten Point of the Deer Clan and new War Chief of Black Bear Village, Two Hearts, warrior of the Wolf Clan, Red Hand, warrior of the Heron Clan and son of Goldeneye, and I believe you have already met Many Feathers and Cold Duck." All were wearing deer or elk robes, making clothing and clan emblems impossible to distinguish.

"We were not introduced to the warriors at the landing, so, no, we did not meet Many Feathers and Cold Duck. Allow me to introduce Yellow Hair. He is from a foreign land but was adopted into the Turtle Clan in Sun Town in the Lenape Nation. Yellow Hair has not fully learned the Monongahela dialect and will have little to say. We are on our way to Cahokia on the Grandfather River. We will stop for a few days in Monongahela Village." Traveler looked only at Night Owl as he spoke.

She humbly replied, "Many Feathers, of the Hawk Clan, is the tall one, and Cold Duck, of the Heron Clan, is the short one. I apologize for their rudeness. We were not expecting visitors. Travel on these swollen rivers is quite treacherous. I am surprised to meet a trader out and about." The last was more of a question.

"I could say the same for your situation. I assume you have important business to conduct or have just completed it," Traveler said. He wanted to stay in charge of the conversation, so he changed the subject. "We have a fresh deer quarter. Maybe your people could get that cooking while Yellow Hair and I set up our shelter? It feels like another cold night. It should be warming up this late in the Awakening Moon." Traveler kept his tone friendly.

"And we have a few fresh-killed ducks and some hominy," Red Loon interjected. "Let us get this feast started!"

Red Hand and Two Hearts pitched in to help Traveler and Yellow Hair get their tent set up. While they did, the wind shifted to the west, then southwest. When the camp was ready for evening meal, the temperature had moderated, taking some of the bite from the wind.

After the meal, Night Owl said to Traveler, "I suppose you are curious about what happened to our previous Great War Chief and why we are going to Monongahela Village on this treacherous river. And we are all quite interested to find out about your foreign friend. There will be much talk about all these things in Corn Stalk's longhouse. But we can give each other a brief story about each subject.

CHAPTER 34

BLACK BEAR VILLAGE

"Two Hearts was present and witnessed the downfall of our past Great War Chief. He will give you a short description of what he saw and heard." Night Owl gestured to the plain-looking warrior.

Yellow Hair noted that when the indicated warrior stood and faced Traveler and himself, Many Feathers rolled his eyes and turned to Cold Duck with an arrogant look on his face. Red Hand gave Two Hearts his full attention, as did Night Owl. Red Loon, Golden Eye, and Ten Point looked bored and distracted. Yellow Hair had to concentrate on what Night Owl was saying, and still missed much of what the Head Matron had to say.

Traveler spoke before Two Hearts began. "I will

need to translate some words for Yellow Hair, so please take that into account, Two Hearts."

"I will do as you wish, trader," Two Hearts replied.

"I, Two Hearts, was one of six scouts sent ahead by the Great War Chief to look for the 'witches' we were hunting. You will learn more of that in the village." He paused for Traveler to tell Yellow Hair what was said.

"Keep it brief, Two Hearts," Night Owl reminded him.

"I heard some bird calls to the northeast as I neared the top of Rock Ridge. As I strained to see if there was some odd activity in that direction, everything suddenly went black. I woke some time later, tied and gagged so that I could not move or talk. A young woman, one of the witches we were hunting, stood over me. She told me she would untie my feet and we would take a little walk. She wore plain hunting clothes, her hair loose and a large chert knife in her hand.

"As my senses returned, I could smell blood and the offal of death close by. She helped me to my feet but held the chert blade to my ribs. She told me to do exactly as she said and nothing more. I nodded eagerly, wishing to stay alive.

"We started up the trail to the northeast at the top of the ridge. To the side, I saw the Second War

Chief lying on his back with a red and black arrow through his throat. I looked up at the sun and determined it was just past midday. It was warm, and as we walked by his corpse, clouds of flies rose, circled, and resettled on the pool of blood around him. I noted that the woman's quiver contained several of those black and red arrows.

"She guided me to a thicket of white cedar shrubs close to a circular clearing. A call from a wood thrush issued from right behind my ear, where the woman held that knife against my back.

"'Do not move a muscle,' she warned me as she guided me to my knees. I froze in the thicket, screened from the clearing, but still able to see into it. "You will live to tell the Black Bears exactly what happened here this day, warrior," she hissed in my ear.

"'I am Pena. In a few heartbeats, my sister, Cass, will guide your war chief into that clearing. They will fight to the death, as ordained by Wolf— First Man,' she said.

"I caught movement and watched my war chief walk into the clearing. He had a big smile on his face and his right hand on the handle of his big war club. A girl followed him, about five paces back. She had a strong-looking bow drawn, with one of those black and red arrows nocked.

"She was a strange looking one. She wore a

gray and brown-streaked hunting shirt, leggings, and moccasins. Her head had been shaved and completely painted with the same colors as her clothes. If she were standing against a chinquapin with her eyes closed, it would be difficult to know she was there. I wondered if that was how she got the advantage on the war chief.

"On her order, the war chief turned and faced her. I could hear her speak. She told the war chief that her spirit helper, Wolf—First Man, ordered her to face her enemy and fight to the death with war clubs. She honored the spirit by arranging this meeting. She relaxed her bow and laid it, with her quiver, on a large rock just outside the clearing.

"She took up her war club. I had never seen one like it. It was made from a dark, orange-colored wood with dark-brown grain patterns. The top end was forked, with a white rock lashed into it. The whole thing was about the length of a forearm.

"She slowly approached the middle of the clearing in a fighting stance. Some words were exchanged that I could not hear. The war chief laughed and set his war club against a tree. With a predatory smile on his face, he approached her. He apparently thought he could catch her, and by the bulge in his breechclout, it looked as if he had other plans.

"She stared at his face with a serious look in her eyes. Suddenly he charged her, but she simply sidestepped him as he went by. On his third charge, she slapped him on the bottom with the side of her club as he zipped past her. After several more failed attempts to capture her, he became frustrated and angry. His forehead was beaded with sweat, hers was not.

"The next two hands of time were like none I have ever seen. Time after time, the war chief charged, swinging his mighty war club in every direction and manner. She evaded every attack without even a scratch. He furiously attacked her, only to miss each attempt to injure her. It was as if she knew his moves before he did. All afternoon, the pursuit went on. He chased and swung his club at her, and she ducked, dipped, jumped, and zipped out of harm's way every time. Both were wearing down, but he was much more fatigued than she.

"At last, she ducked and plunged in with her club drawn back. He swung his club down, trying to hit her shoulder. But she had already retreated, and his club struck the ground hard, sending a shockwave up his arm. A heartbeat later, she did the same move. This time, when his club was committed to striking the ground, she transferred her club to her left hand and slammed that white rock into the back of his hand. I could hear the bones breaking in his hand as they were crushed. He screamed in pain and backed up.

"A short time later, she had him lying on the ground, crippled. Once the war chief was on the ground, the young woman warrior let out a red-shouldered hawk screech. The one with the knife to my back ushered me into the clearing. She ordered me to sit against a small elm tree at the edge, tied me to it, and bound my feet together. I did not even notice the bags she had picked up from somewhere.

"The war chief was barely alive and in more pain than any man could endure. His knees and elbows were crushed, and he had an arrow through his testicles, pinning his buttocks to the ground. It was difficult to look at him.

"The one who fought the war chief went to the edge of the slope and started a fire, then placed white cedar boughs on it to signal to our warriors that the war chief was destroyed. I could see he still breathed, though.

"The two women left me tied to the tree and disappeared over the ridge to the south. Before the Black Bear warriors arrived, the war chief had vomited, choked, and was barely alive. There was nothing I could do.

"It has been less than a moon since that day,

but the images I witnessed haunt my dreams each night. At the same time, I can admit that what those young women did was beyond belief but justified. The war chief was a bad man who ruled Black Bear Village with fear and intimidation," Two Hearts concluded, looking at his feet.

"That account was more detailed than we wanted to hear, Two Hearts," Night Owl admonished.

"I am not sad that the warrior told as he did," Yellow Hair spoke up.

Night Owl looked at him, astonished. "We were led to believe you do not know our tongue," she replied with skepticism in her voice.

"At first, but Two Hearts make easier as he talk slow. Yellow Hair hear gooder and gooder. Traveler not need say words of the last parts at all," Yellow Hair answered.

CHAPTER 35

ROUGH RIVER

After a break and a stretch, Traveler said, "Yellow Hair's story involves many things we are not able to comprehend, so I will be brief. We can get to Monongahela Village early tomorrow, but we need all the sleep we can get because the rivers will be treacherous."

"Do go on with Yellow Hair's story, trader. I am eager to hear how this foreigner musters the courage to walk among real people," Many Feathers interjected with disdain in his voice.

Night Owl interrupted, "Many Feathers! You will not be rude to our guests! Perhaps I should have chosen another warrior to paddle a canoe? Maybe we should leave you here while we do our business in Monongahela Village."

"Many Feathers will respect the foreigner when he earns it. Many Feathers must meet the young woman, Cass. I will show her how a true warrior behaves and make her my wife. No foreigner will interfere with my plans," the tall warrior replied in defiance.

"Many Feathers, Yellow Hair not here for maiden. Traveler and Yellow Hair must go Cahokia. After that, only spirits know, but no woman is plan. Woman sounds dangerous, but if she no want you, Yellow Hair help woman. No woman should marry a man she does not want," Yellow Hair said in answer to Many Feathers's challenge.

"Enough! We will hear no more from young men with swollen manhoods and small brains. Traveler, please tell Yellow Hair's story in words we can comprehend. Then we will turn in. It will be a long day tomorrow, regardless of the river conditions," Night Owl declared.

"Yes, Head Matron." Traveler told Yellow Hair's life story, trying to describe the Norse ways in words that the people present could understand. The description of great canoes that could hold a whole village and fly across the Great Eastern Ocean, pushed by the wind using a huge blanket that looked like an eagle's wing drew much skepticism.

Yellow Hair's survival on a raft made of one board after many days at sea was met with sympathy, awe, and disbelief. They were convinced he was no god. But he was here, and no one could offer a better explanation as to how it had happened.

With many unanswered questions still hanging, Night Owl declared it was time for sleep. The winds had died, and the air had warmed and become quite humid. Clouds obscured the stars and moon.

The morning turned out even warmer and more humid. A dense fog hung everywhere without the slightest hint of a breeze. At first light, it was difficult to count fingers on a hand at the end of an outstretched arm. People had to talk to identify who was who in the camp. A delayed departure was unwanted but necessary. A crackling fire barely produced an orange glow just a couple of paces from the flames.

In a hand of time, the fog had barely lifted enough to see the river. However, all were anxious to break the damp camp and be on their way. Traveler knew the rivers best, so his canoe was elected to lead. Until they reached the Monongahela, the rest would follow him, single file. He would guide them across that river, but he and Yellow Hair would allow the Black Bear Villagers to arrive at Monongahela Village first.

Tent coverings had to be rolled inside out because everything was so wet. It took another hand of time to pack up the camp due to the wetness of everything that had not been under cover. A few arguments broke out when one person wanted to perform a task differently than another person did, or someone got wet due to someone else fumbling one task or another. Eventually all the equipment and people were loaded in the canoes, and they were ready to shove off.

They had little trouble crossing the Kiskiminetas River. Going down the east bank of the Spirit Water was a challenge, however. They had to stick close to shore, where the smoothest water was, and they were constantly being scraped and brushed by branches and the limbs of trees lining the riverbank. Some of those trees and brush were submerged, and usually, the canoes just floated over them. Often enough, however, the hidden woody vegetation caused the craft to wobble or get turned unexpectedly. That submerged woody material also waved and undulated with the current, making things more unpredictable.

Finally, they approached the confluence of the

Spirit Water and Monongahela. Where the two currents collided, huge waves were thrown up, rolled over, crashed, and splashed. Whole trees carried by the river currents sometimes collided in that churning mess. Such occasions caused the most intrepid canoeist to cower. The river levels were high enough that the point of land on the east was partially submerged.

Traveler artfully led them through the flooded timber to a point upstream from the confluence where the bank was higher than the water. He signaled that they needed to move farther upstream.

Yellow Hair was impressed with Traveler's skills. He was learning everything he could about traveling on overflowing rivers. He was also getting tired. The short time they had been on the river this morning had been exhausting and stressful, and it was not over yet. Supposedly, Monongahela Village was just across the river. But the fog had cut the visibility to about one-half the river's width. Yellow Hair surmised that because the edge of the fogbank hovered right down the middle of the flotsam that was concentrated in the center of the river.

He was getting anxious to get to the village. Despite his comments the night before, his interest was piqued in the warrior girl, Cass. He pictured her as a muscle-bound freak with a shaved head. He imagined a broad face and hard, squinty eyes.

Traveler jerked him back to reality when he put the canoe into a hard turn to the left. Looking up, Yellow Hair saw a large tree trunk floating right at them. He drove his paddle deep into the water and pulled with all his might. After three hard strokes the log barely bumped their right side. As the tree drifted past them, Yellow Hair could see that the bigger limbs had already been broken off. Traveler shouted a warning to the crew behind them and exhaled a sigh of relief when Cold Duck and Many Feathers, last in line, passed the deadly obstacle.

There was no change in the land, current, or weather when Traveler announced it was time to cut for the south bank of the river. The experienced trader advised that they would turn and run with the current, gradually moving through the flotsam and to the far riverbank. Traveler and Yellow Hair would land on the far bank and wait a hand of time while the others proceeded to the village and landed.

All five canoes made it across to the south bank without incident, but right after the others set out downriver, Yellow Hair caught movement. In the center of the flotsam, the water roiled. Suddenly, a whole tree, with several broken, but not separated, limbs thrust up out of the water, rolled, and sank back underwater. A few seconds later, the root system heaved out, and the tree rolled, and sank into the water again. Yellow Hair wondered how many times that tree would roll before it was reduced to splinters..

CHAPTER 36
RED HAND

Waiting to shove off again, Yellow Hair's thoughts drifted to the girl, Cass, and a conversation he had with Red Hand. Red Hand was planning to marry Cass's sister, the one called Pena. Yellow Hair had learned that Red Hand was born in Long Pine Village. He was eight summers old when he was captured. His mother was made a sex slave of the Great War Chief while Red Hand was forced into Goldeneye's clan. His mother had resisted the warriors that used her and was tortured to death. Red Hand was eventually adopted into the Heron Clan and became a man.

Before Red Hand earned his adult name, which could only happen by killing an enemy warrior or a big male bear, the "boy" was out hunting in a late snow and ran across some bear tracks. He was following along cautiously when he heard a bear growl, then cry out, as if in pain, then a muffled crash. Carefully, he made his way toward the sounds. There, a hundred paces ahead, was the bear, apparently dead, laying in bloody, red snow.

Red Hand said he went up to offer his assistance to whomever had killed the bear. The tracks led to a spreading chestnut tree near the abandoned Long Pine Village. When he looked up the tree, expecting to see a hunter, he was surprised when he was confronted by a beautiful girl pointing an arrow at his chest. Despite the threatening posture, he offered to help her with the bear. He learned she was called Pena.

As they dragged the bear to where her canoe was beached, he learned she had a *friend* who turned out to be her twin sister. It was there that he met Cass. They were so close in appearance he could only tell them apart by the clothes they wore that day. She came out of nowhere, also pointing an arrow at his chest. The three had a long conversation, with Pena agreeing to meet him again. Cass still wanted to kill him.

Over the next couple of sun cycles, Red Hand earned his man status by killing an Owasco raider. He and Pena fell in love but kept it a secret from everyone except Cass. He agreed to be their spy in Black Bear Village.

He had known the girls when they were small, back in Long Pine Village, but with everything that happened, he had blocked out the memories of his life before he had been taken to Black Bear Village. Now, he and Pena wanted a future together. If he could help bring an end to Great War Chief Thunder Throat, he would. It would be risky, but Pena was worth any risk.

Then, Goldeneye became Head Matron of the Heron Clan. She needed an alliance with the Bear Clan, so she arranged a marriage between Red Hand and one of Night Owl's granddaughters. He would be locked in a clan marriage and never able to fulfill his dream of marrying Pena. Both were heartbroken but continued the liaisons in the woods whenever they could. It was difficult, at best. As a cover, he pretended to be a loyal follower of the Great War Chief, and somehow the lovers never got caught.

Cass came up with a plan to draw the Great War Chief to her by pretending she and Pena were witches. She and Pena wore costumes and hid on hunting trails. They would appear only to the Great War Chief's most loyal warriors at strategic times and injure them. The story was enhanced when two Black Bear Village hunters had disappeared near the old Long Pine Village site. Shortly after that, the first "witch" story emerged.

Things became complicated when Red Hand's wife became pregnant. It looked as if Red Hand and Pena would never get to be together.

Winter came and the "witches" struck again, breaking the knees of two of the Great War Chief's seconds. He made plans for a war walk. He was convinced the "witches" were the two girls he planned to capture and enslave, along with their aunt, when he raided and destroyed Long Pine Village. Somehow the three girls had escaped his clutches and evaded him for nine sun cycles. The Great War Chief was now convinced they were being harbored and aided by Corn Stalk in Monongahela Village. His war walk would destroy the Head Matron of the Monongahela People if she did not turn the "witches" over to him.

"The day before we were to depart on the war walk, a heavy snowfall hit. The snow made it impossible to travel, and the Great War Chief was livid. When the weather finally broke, we started on the war walk. Two Hearts told you how that turned out.

"Also, my wife's time to give birth came while that blizzard was raging. She and the baby died in the women's lodge. I was not able to feel much remorse, I must admit. I did not have any feelings for her and did not want a child with her. I only consummated the marriage to fulfill a clan obligation," Red Hand had explained. "Now, I am on my way to see if Pena will still take me."

"I wish you luck," Yellow Hair had said.

———

"ARE you ready for some more river adventure?" Traveler asked Yellow Hair, breaking his reverie. The memory of his conversation with Red Hand while they waited for the fog to lift had rekindled his interest in the young woman called Cass.

"Not until I shed some of these clothes," Yellow Hair answered, realizing how warm it had gotten. In a few heartbeats, he shed his heavy buckskin leggings and shirt. He put on just a vest, tied over his sternum with a thong. He kept his breechclout with its fringed apron and Turtle Clan images and his moccasins. When he settled into the canoe and looked down, he was shocked at how white his legs appeared. It had been at least four moons since those legs had seen sunlight.

"We should make the landing in about a hand of time, maybe less in that current. It will be on your left side, right after a large willow that may be partially submerged in this high water. Right after that willow, we will bear left and find an opening among the other canoes," Traveler instructed.

"With the river this high, will we be able to see the village from the water?" Yellow Hair asked.

"Perhaps. The palisade may be shielded from view by trees. We should see smoke from hearth fires, but those low clouds may make smoke hard to see," the trader answered. The fog had lifted to about the treetops along the river bottom.

As they drifted downriver, mostly using their paddles only to steer, they kept a sharp eye out for snags, sawyers, and other hazards in the fast-moving water while Yellow Hair kept one eye on the south side of the river. It had been rather plain, just a gentle bend, then almost straight as far downstream as he could see. There was a narrow band of reeds and rushes mixed with willow brush and occasional bigger trees along the riverbank. Obviously, the high water changed the appearance. He suspected that under normal conditions, he would be looking at a bare-mud bank more than three times higher than a man.

He scanned the forest south of the river for signs of civilization, and saw only a few, what looked like, trails. At last, he thought he could see smoke rising in thin columns into the sky. The palisade was completely obscured by trees. Suddenly, every patch of open ground was worked into little hills to plant corn. A team of women, young girls, and boys were working with digging sticks, planting corn seeds in one of the fields.

"Just ahead is the landing," Traveler pointed to the big willow, its base under water. Through the brush to the south of the tree, Yellow Hair thought he made out a small group of people gathered. Suddenly, they were past the tree and the land curved in a large arc into the south bank. There must have been more than five hundred canoes laying on the bank. The river in the area was right at the top of the bank.

Turning into the shallow bay, Yellow Hair noted a person had broken from the group of people and was hurdling the overturned canoes. It was a feminine figure, moving with the grace of a deer bounding through a forest of deadfalls.

A LOOK AT BOOK THREE
CASS

In a tale of epic vengeance and personal transformation, one Norse warrior's quest for justice and redemption unfolds.

At only eight years old, Cass's world is shattered when she witnesses the brutal murder and mutilation of her parents by the ruthless war chief Thunder Throat and his marauding forces. Orphaned and consumed by a quest for vengeance, she finds solace and guidance from a powerful spirit, her twin sister, and a devoted extended family.

As the years pass, Cass endures rigorous training, driven by an unyielding desire to reclaim her lost world and avenge the unspeakable wrongs committed against her family. Her journey takes her from the haunting ruins of her village to a fateful battle against the greatest warrior of her time.

Despite the doubts of her elders and the relentless dangers she faces, Cass remains resolute in her mission to defeat the Great War Chief. With everything on the line, she will stop at nothing to embrace her destiny and restore justice to her world.

Embark on an unforgettable journey of courage and resolve.

AVAILABLE NOVEMBER 2024

ABOUT THE AUTHOR

Ron Briggs is a veteran, having served four years in the USAF. His education includes a Bachelor of Science in Range and Wildlife Ecology at Oklahoma State University and a Master of Science in Range and Wildlife Management at Texas A&I University.

He is retired from the USDA-Natural Resources Conservation Service, and his career encompassed twenty-five years as District Conservationist in Linn County, Kansas. Prior to college, he worked seven years in the building trades.

Having developed a deep interest in history, especially in the pre-colonial period of North America, Ron's interests prompted him to begin researching a pre-history story about the Tallgrass Prairie Region of the Great Plains. That research evolved into his current multi-volume work, the Yellow Hair series, which includes scenes from northern Europe to the mountains of western North America.

Ron and his wife, Debbie, currently live in Mound City, Kansas, and have two grown children and seven grandchildren. His interests include spending time with family, writing, hunting, fishing, traveling, and woodworking.

BIBLIOGRAPHY

Appelt, Martin. "Man, Culture and Environment in Ancient Greenland." *Publication No. 4*, Danish Polar Center 1998.

Bierhorst, John. *Mythology of the Lanape: Guide and Texts*. University of Arizona Press, 1995.

Bronsted, Johannes. *The Vikings*. Penguin Books, 1960, rev ed. 1965.

Charles River Editors. *Native American Tribes: The History and Culture of the Innuit (Eskimos)*. 2013.

Clarke, Helen and Bjorn Ambrosiani. *Towns in the Viking Age*. St. Martin's Press, 1991.

Cohat, Yves, tr. Daniel, Ruth. *The Vikings: Lords of the Seas*. Gallimard 1987.

Damas, David and William C. Sturtevant, eds.1984. *Handbook of North American Indians Vol. 5-Arctic*. Smithsonian Press, 1985.

Feasel, Charles T. *White Bear*. Ballantine, 1990.

Fitzhugh, William and Elizabeth Ward. *Vikings, The North Atlantic Saga*. Smithsonian Press, 2000.

Gordon,E. V., rev by Taylor, A. R. *An Introduction to Old Norse*. Oxford University Press, 1956.

Gronnow, Bjarni. "Late Dorset in High Arctic Greenland: Final Report on the Gateway to Greenland Project." Canadian Archeological Association, 1999.

Grumet, Robert S. *The Lenapes (Indians of North America)*. Chelsea House, 1989.

Harrington, Mark R. *Religion and Ceremonies of the Lenape*. Forgotten Books, 2012.

--. *The Indians of New Jersey, Dickon Among the Lenapes*. Rutgers University Press, 1963.

Heckewelder, John Gotlieb Ernestus, notes by William C.

Reichel. "History, Manners, and Customs of The Indian Nations Who Inhabited Pennsylvania and the Neighbouring States." Historical Society of Pennsylvania, 1881.

Ingstad, Anne Stine, et al. "The Discovery of a Norse Settlement in America. Excavations at L'Anse aux Meadows, Newfoundland, 1961-1968." Tromso, 1977.

Jones, Gwynne. *A History of the Vikings*. Oxford University Press, 1984.

Kunz, Keneva, tr., ed. Gisli Sigurdsson. *The Vinland Sagas*. Penguin, 2008.

McCullough, K. M. "The Ruin Islanders: Thule Culture Pioneers in the High Eastern Arctic." *Archeological Survey of Canada*, 141, Canadian Museum of Civilization. 1989.

McGee, Robert. *Ancient People of the Arctic*. University of British Columbia Press, 1996.

--. *The Last Imaginary Place*. Oxford University Press, 2005.

Mcleod, William Christie. "The Family Hunting Territory and Lenape Political Organization." *American Anthropology 24*, 1922.

Maschner, Herbert; Owen Masson, Robert McGee. *The Northern World AD 900-1400*. University of Utah Press, 2009.

Maxwell, Moreau S. *Prehistory of the Eastern Arctic*. Academic Press, 1985.

Means, Bernard K. *Circular Villages of the Monongahela Tradition*. University of Alabama Press, 2007.

Rasmusen, Knud. *Eskimo Folk Tales*. Gyldendal, (Copenhagen), 1921.

Roesdahl, Else. *The Vikings*. Penguin, 1987.

Schledermann, Peter. *Crossroads to Greenland, 3000 Years of Prehistory in the Eastern High Arctic*. The Arctic Institute of North America of the University of Calgary, 1990.

Seaver, Kirsten A. *The Frozen Echo, Greenland and the Exploration of North America, ca. A.D. 1000-1500*. Stanford University Press, 1996.

BIBLIOGRAPHY

Simpson, Jacqueline. *Everyday Life in the Viking Age*. Dorset Press, 1967.

Sutherland, Patricia, ed. "Contributions to the Study of Dorset Paleo Eskimos." Canada Museum of History, 2005.

Trigger, Bruce G. *Handbook of North American Indians, Volume 15-Northeast*. Smithsonian Press, 1984.

Weslager, C. A. *The Delaware Indians: A History*. Rutgers University Press, 1972.